WHEN EVIL REIGNS SUPREME

RICH SIEGEL

www. MaxMillerNovels.com

Majestic Mystery Publishers
Cover by Jeff Shelley
(reelhead@gmail.com)

Copyright © 2008 by Rich Siegel

ISBN:978-0-578-03216-0

ABOUT THE AUTHOR

Despite the prodding of his high school English teachers and college professors, Rich Siegel chose not to pursue a career in writing, choosing instead the safe, secure and "utterly monotonous" world of accounting. Alas, the author within could take it no longer, resulting in his first novel, *A Matter of Distance*.

He is currently working on his third novel, the sequel to *When Evil Reigns Supreme*. A self-proclaimed golf addict, the native Long Islander recently put to rest his dream of going on tour as a PGA professional, his eighteen handicap playing a major role in his decision.

Dedicated to the loving memory of my dad, "Big Al" Siegel.

PROLOGUE

His First Victim - Alisha Marizzo

When I was still a kid in high school, my buddies and I used to get quite a thrill from our leisurely little rides through the well-hidden neighborhoods of Muttontown, Long Island. Ever so slowly, we'd cruise down those narrow, winding roads, where overhanging trees blocked out much of the sky above, as we'd "ooh" and "aah" at the sight of stately mansions, standing proudly alone, atop acres and acres of beautifully designed landscapes.

On that late spring evening some thirty-five years later, I found myself gazing out upon those very same homes. No longer, however, was I able to envision their grandiose living rooms or posh, formal dining rooms, exquisitely garnished in the very finest of décor. All that I could see, as we quickly passed them by, were the dark, vacant hallways above. Pitch-black corridors adorned in row upon row of tightly shut doors. Hidden, in dead silence, behind those doors lay the blank emptiness within.

I had never regretted my decision to become a cop until that very evening. It was then that I told my partner and closest comrade, Claude Greer, that if I could have somehow known that such an evening would one day arrive then I would have chosen a different way to earn a living as a banker or plumber or anything at all, but not as a homicide detective on his way to a home where, in the wink of an eye, a little girl's bedroom had been so brutally transformed into a museum of memories, far too painful to behold.

CHAPTER 1

Five weeks after the Alisha Marizzo murder

The knock on my door was so faint and my vision so distorted by my reading glasses that I wasn't able to tell for sure if there was even anyone there. My sharp police mind, however, allowed me to solve this dilemma in a flash. So off came the glasses.

There she was, standing in the doorway, a most sacred of sights to behold. The sheer presence of her soothing, pale-brown face and exquisite hour-glass anatomy might very well have caused the staunchest of atheists to, momentarily, question their lack of belief.

"Can I help you?" I asked without further delay.

"Good morning, Detective Miller. My name's Lisa Sanchez," she replied, her voice barely louder than a whisper.

So I went ahead and asked her if she'd like to have a seat.

She thanked me for offering and then, slowly, walked towards me.

As she leaned forward, to sit herself down on the steel-framed chair across from me, I snuck a quick, inconspicuous glance at her invigorating exterior. But then, the very second that her derriere lay flush upon the seat of the chair, those mind-numbing words flew out of her mouth.

"I know what he looks like, Detective."

Just like that, her ravishing allure disappeared into thin air. What sat before me now was nothing more than a messenger, one that sparkled with a glimmer of hope and salvation.

I cleared the nervous tickle from my throat and stared straight into her big, brown eyes.

Then, in a calm and soothing voice, I asked, "Do you know *who* he is?"

"No," was all she said.

With my hands clasped in front of me and my eyes still locked into hers, I sat there, patiently waiting for her to continue until her silence became too much for me to bear.

"Then how do you know what he looks like?"

1

"He appears in my dreams, the night before he murders."

"Well, ain't that just dandy," that little voice in my head screamed, as my brief moment of hope that this could be the lead that we'd so desperately been waiting for plunged faster than a two-ton anchor.

"So how may I be of assistance to you, Ms. Sanchez?"

"I'd like to help you catch him."

My phony little grin camouflaged the intense frustration within as I handed her a sheet of memo paper, upon which I asked her to jot down her name and phone number. After she honored my request, I folded up the sheet of paper and placed it in my wallet, to make it look as though it was actually worth something to me.

Then I stood up, waited for her to follow suit and escorted her to the door.

"I'll be in touch," I said.

"Thank you, Detective," she replied, as she gently returned my handshake.

Then she turned and walked out the door.

I stood there watching her as she wiggled her way down the hallway. When she turned the corner, I headed back to my desk and sat back down on that hard-as-a-rock desk chair of mine. I amused myself by thinking that the odds of my early morning mystery guest helping us catch this no-good-piece-of-scum were right up there with me hitting the lottery for a couple of hundred mil on the same day that I'm walking down the aisle for a third time.

Then I slipped my reading glasses back on and got back to the grind of the growing pile of paperwork that I'd been putting off for way too long.

CHAPTER 2

He stared straight ahead, through the small square hole in the center of the maze's brick wall, his lips pressed together, so not even a peep could sneak through them. Right there in front of him stood a little girl with long, auburn hair and eyes a tad shade lighter than the crystal-blue sky above.

Round and round she hopped on the hot, black pavement, the warm glow of her bright, wide smile gently illuminating her entire being; fitting proof of her often-mentioned claim that the playground was her favorite place to be in the whole, entire world.

As the minutes quickly passed, his thrill derived in watching her each and every move slowly began to simmer. He knew all too well that the dreaded task of admitting defeat to the others was growing more and more likely.

But then, luck took a swift and sudden turn in his direction: Mother had just turned around and run in desperate pursuit of the little girl's pint-sized sibling.

Quickly, he zigzagged his way out of the maze.

Now, in plain view of the playful child, he sat kneeling like a catcher, ready for the next pitch.

"Psst, little girl, do you want to play in the maze?"

The little girl abruptly stopped and took a long, slow look at him. Then, with a smile so innocent sprawled across her pretty little face, she hopped up and down towards the soft-spoken man.

"Atta girl, come on, you're almost there," he whispered.

When at last she came within his grasp, he sprang forward and cupped his hand over her mouth. Without wasting a moment's time, he threw her over his shoulder and took off, full speed, towards the opening in the tall, arched bushes. He raced onward until he reached his destination: a small, black car, well hidden amidst the dense shrubbery. In one swift motion, he flung open the passenger door, threw the little girl inside and shuffled himself over her to get to the driver's seat.

As he sped away, a barrage of tears began to flow down the little girl's face. But she just sat there and let them drench her, too frozen with fear to wipe them away. Fixated on the road

3

ahead, he drove on and on, not once looking over at the sobbing young child sitting beside him.

Upon exiting the expressway some fifty minutes later, he drove down the deserted country roads of Eastern Suffolk County for quite some time. Eventually, he pulled his car off the road and drove through the tall weeds, in the direction of the woods beyond. When he got to the woods, he stopped his car for a brief moment and then proceeded along at a snail's pace, eyeballing each and every tree that he passed.

When at last, he came upon a tree of his liking, he shut off the engine and stepped out of the car.

With his right hand cupped over his eyes to block out the breaks of sunlight, he looked hard at his surroundings. Seeing that all appeared safe, he clicked open the trunk and pulled out a metal folding table and a long, gray rope with a noose tied into place. He tossed the metal table on the ground, grabbed hold of the rope and then hurried to the front of the car.

With rope in hand, he jumped onto the hood of the car and then hopped onto the roof. From there, he threw the rope over the tree's low-lying branch and tied it tightly into place. A warm rush shot through his body as he glanced down at the noose dangling in midair.

Quickly, he slid inside the car through the open window and backed it up a few short yards.

After kicking away the dry leaves, he snapped open the table and placed it down on the leveled ground. He pressed the palm of his hands down upon it to make sure that it stood sturdy. Then, he hurried back to his car, grabbed the little girl by her arms and dragged her over to the table.

"Ow," she screamed, as he yanked her up and onto the tall, metal table.

Face up and motionless, she lay.

He stood over her, smirking as he unraveled the thin string that lay nestled around his left hand. With methodic precision, he wrapped the string around her wrists and tied them tightly to the legs of the table. Then, in this same robotic manner, he repeated the process on her ankles.

To mark the commencement of his beloved little ceremony, he pulled a small, red camera out of his pants pocket, took a few backward steps and snapped a photo of his subject. Then he stepped forward, leaned over the little girl and stared straight into her light blue eyes, his piercing brown eyes bulging with excitement.

"Now you will repeat my words, my child. Do you understand?"

The little girl nodded her head, just barely, and then did as she was told.

"Please forgive me, Dear God, for thinking myself worthy of you. My sheepish pleas for mercy have disgraced you. So, please, Dear Lord, cut away the soul of Satan that possesses me and release him from my being."

Later on, he ended his ceremony by cutting loose the strings that secured her to the table and kicking the legs out from under it, causing the little girl to hang in midair, semi-conscious, with the toes of her feet vehemently struggling to touch the ground.

When her struggle was over, he stood there, proudly admiring his efforts. Then he folded up the metal table, laid it gently into the trunk of his car and slowly drove away.

CHAPTER 3

I've been worshiping the fairways of the Eagle Crest Golf Club on Saturday afternoons for quite a number of years now. It's the one place where I can stop playing homicide detective for a little while.

Well, usually, that is.

As I was lining up a putt on the Saturday that followed Lisa Sanchez's visit to my office, my cell phone started ringing. It sounded like taps to my ears. Why? Because no one ever calls me when I'm on the links except for one person - my good-ole-partner-against-crime, Claude Greer. Of those few calls that he's made, not one was to express good news and cheer.

So I did a fast sprint to my golf cart and grabbed my phone out of the glove box.

"Hello" I said, breathing somewhat heavily from lack of oxygen.

"Max. He's struck again. Her name was Melissa O'Leary. Poor kid was only four."

A bolt of adrenaline rushed through me as I tightened my grip on my putter and then wound up and slammed it into the roof of my golf cart. *Smack!*

"You, OK? Max, are you OK?" I heard my partner's voice screaming through the phone.

"I'm just wonderful," I screamed back. *"Another little girl. I'm just fucking wonderful."*

"We'll catch this motherfucker, Max. Believe me, we will."

"Yeah, when? When the fuck are we gonna catch him?"

I clicked off the phone without giving Claude a chance to answer. I was in no mood whatsoever for empty reassurances, well intented or not. Through the corner of my eye, I caught sight of my golf buddies hurrying towards me but I waved them off rather emphatically.

Frustrated beyond mercy, I leaned against my golf cart and tossed my cell phone into the open glove box. A moment or two later, without giving a lot of thought as to what I was doing, I pulled out my wallet and took out the sheet of memo paper with Lisa Sanchez's phone number on it. Then I reached over

6

and picked my phone back up.

Desperation had just hit a new all-time low.

CHAPTER 4

I was thrown off guard when she opened her apartment door because she looked much shorter than she did the previous day. I glanced down at her feet. The brown, open-toed sandals that she had on were quite a bit flatter than the black high-heels that she wore to my office; quite a bit more casual-looking as well. The rest of her looked just as casual: blue jeans and a bright red tee shirt that broadcast the words "OLD NAVY" across her well-developed chest. Her long, jet-black hair was tied back in a ponytail; her large, seductive lips were devoid of any lipstick.

"Please come in," she said.

"Thanks very much," I replied, as I stepped inside.

Her apartment was small, real small - a tiny living room and kitchenette area to the left, a bedroom and bathroom to the right. That was it.

"Can I get you something to drink," she asked, as she led me a few steps into her dimly lit living room.

"No, nothing, thanks," I heard myself respond, despite the fact that I was actually kind of thirsty.

I stood in the middle of the room, glancing around at the religious artifacts displayed throughout. A large, wood-framed painting of the Virgin Mary holding the Baby Jesus in her arms, sat centered on the wall over the sofa.

"Please have a seat," she said, motioning to the off-white sofa.

"Mind if I sit there," I asked, pointing to the burgundy crushed-velvet chair directly across from it.

"No, please, by all means, sit wherever you'd like."

Well, I would've *liked* to have sat right on her lap, or vice versa, perhaps, which is precisely why I chose to be a safe distance away. So I sat down on her soft-cushioned chair and got right to the point.

"Ms. Sanchez, this man that you spoke about, could you describe what he looks like?"

"He appeared again, last night."

I nodded my head, but said nothing.

"What I see in these dreams is a vision of this man. It's not

8

a *portrait* of him, but rather a vision."

"Do you see anyone else in these dreams?"

"No, just him."

"Then what is it about him that makes you think he's the killer?"

"I don't know, exactly. I just know that it's him."

"Have you ever had…*premonitions* like this in the past?"

"No. Never."

"Is there anything at all that you can tell me about this vision of a person?"

A silence longer than that at a funeral procession then set in, just like it did the previous day at my office. But this time, just when I was good and ready to give myself a swift kick in the ass out of there, she began to exercise her vocal cords a bit more.

"There *is* something that I think you should know about him, Detective Miller."

"What's that?"

"He's dressed the same in all of the dreams."

She seemed awfully uncomfortable telling me that, as though she was embarrassed to be talking about it for some reason.

"How was he dressed?" I very calmly asked.

Tears began to appear in those big, brown eyes of hers. She closed them and took a deep breath.

"He's dressed in a black shirt with a white collar."

She took another breath and with her eyes still closed, she whispered fiercely, *"He's dressed like a priest, Detective Miller."*

CHAPTER 5

I called Claude as soon as I got back to my car. I wanted to arrange to meet with him as soon as possible. I needed to bounce the little séance session that I had just had with Lisa Sanchez off his chest.

The Greers' answering machine picked up, so, I waited for the annoying little beep as instructed.

"Claude, ole Buddy, ole Pal, being that you ruined my day off, I figured I'd return the favor. Call me when you get this message; it's kind of important. Thanks pudgy-boy."

I threw in the "pudgy-boy" part to give Tamara and Pam, his adorable little kids, something to giggle about; the thought of little girls giggling was a welcome relief from what I'd been exposed to lately.

Claude returned my call before I even had time to get the top down on my Corvette. I told him to meet me at the Gateway Pub in an hour or so, without going into any details. Then, I rolled down the top of my Vette and made my way to the Long Island Expressway.

I was on the Expressway for five minutes at the most, when I started doubting the necessity of my meeting with Claude, just like I knew I would. That, by the way, happens to be the reason why I called him when I did, *before* I had enough time to talk myself out of it. At age fifty-three, I'd gotten to know myself pretty well. In some respects, that is.

Despite my rapidly increasing degree of skepticism, I wasn't about to call off my little meeting with Claude because I knew damn well that we had absolutely nothing to lose at that point. It'd been a case with no clues. That psychopathic piece of crap was making fools out of us. Two police departments assigned to one case and we still had absolutely nothing to go on.

I pulled into the barely-empty parking lot of the Gateway Pub just as Claude was stepping out of his red Ford Explorer. The Gateway happens to be about the same distance from my home in Massapequa as it is from Claude's home in Baldwin. That's one of the reasons why we like to meet there. It's also a fairly big place, so there's never been a problem getting a table where we can talk in confidence.

10

"Pudgy-boy, huh," were the words that Claude used to greet me.

"Did the kids hear it?"

"You bet they did. They got quite a kick out of it."

"That's what I was hoping you'd say," I said as I extended my hand to him. He shook it rather firmly, then released it and put his hand on his belly.

"I think pudgy-*man* would have been a little more respectful, partner. Those days of referring to us black guys as "boy" are long behind us."

"You know something, Claude? You're right. Pudgy-*man* it is."

We exchanged good-natured grins and then headed towards the Gateway's front entrance.

Once inside, we walked over to the bar and ordered a couple of twenty-ounce beers. With beer mugs in hand, we made our way past a long row of tables to the backroom and sat down at a booth in the far left corner of the room.

The place was almost completely empty, which I'm sure it usually was on sunny weekend afternoons in the summertime, when most people on Long Island are spending their time looking at some large body of water, either from one of its beaches or from the deck of someone's boat.

After Claude filled me in on the gruesome details of the Missy O'Leary murder, I gave him the rundown on Lisa Sanchez. He didn't know how to react at first, I could tell. Finally, he said what I pretty much expected him to say.

"We're approaching the desperation zone, huh, Max."

"We're beyond that, Claude. I think we've entered the *Twilight Zone*."

Normally, we would have been laughing pretty heartily over that little one-liner of mine, but not then. Four little girls had been brutally murdered; any tears shared over that were not shed from laughter.

Claude, being every bit as much the skeptic as I, surprised me a little with what he said next.

"I think we should at least do a background check on her. We've got nothing to lose."

As I sat there, contemplating my response, Claude reached over and took a sip of his beer. Then he placed his beer mug down real, real slowly. Through his eyes, I could see that his brain had just shifted into high gear.

"If you think about it, Max, a priest might actually fit in pretty well here."

"Why's that?"

"Because every parent that we spoke with told us that their daughters were taught repeatedly never to approach a stranger. Not one of them could believe for a second that their kid would voluntarily walk over to someone that they didn't know, yet every one of the kids seems to have done so."

"That seems to be the general consensus."

"So, what would a priest or someone posing as one, represent to a four-or-five-year-old Catholic girl? A person of trust, right?"

"How do you know that they were all Catholic?"

"I don't, but if I were to venture a guess, I'd say they probably were because none of them had Jewish-sounding last names. Around here, it's usually one or the other. That's certainly not the case in Middle America but around here it sure is."

"As you well know, you're talking to the son of a Catholic mother and Jewish father, so I know exactly what you're saying. And the girls' religion will be easy enough for us to find out. But first, like you said, let's see what the computers have to say about this Lisa Sanchez character."

Claude responded with those all too familiar words.

"We've got nothing to lose."

Thus far, such words would have made a fitting name for the title song of our investigation. We knew damn well, though, that we owed it to all the little girls on Long Island to change it to something like "All is safe, once again, our little ones."

That song could not be sung, however, until we found that someone or something that could help us compose it.

CHAPTER 6

When I arrived home from the Gateway Pub, my big, furry bundle of happiness, Sparky, was at the front door, waiting to greet me. Good old Sparky is my best friend. Through thick and thin, he's always there with his long, brown tail wagging back and forth like a whip. No human has ever been so thrilled to see me, day in and day out. That's for damn sure.

My live-in lover, Kerri, was out doing her usual 5 to 2 shift at the strip joint where she works. It might seem unusual to some for a cop to be living with an exotic dancer, but to me it made perfect sense. Especially after considering what my first two wives were like.

With Kerri, everything was so nice and simple. We'd eat some meals together, watch some TV together and screw like a couple of canines in heat as often as possible. All that, with no commitments and a minimal amount of petty arguments. Now what could possibly be better than that?

Some might argue that it's too shallow because it lacks that little four-letter word, but for someone like me that stuff only existed in the world of fiction, like in movies and novels. It wasn't part of my vocabulary and hadn't been for a long, long time.

I took Sparky for a leisurely stroll around the block and then stopped by the kitchen to grab a can of beer from the refrigerator. Then I headed to the living room, plopped down in my easy chair and clicked on the video of the Yankee game that I had recorded. As is usually the case, however, I started dozing off way before the game was over. Damn games are way too long these days.

I decided to shower before retiring for the night because, dollars to doughnuts, Kerri would be waking me when she got home. Eight hours of exposing her naked body to a countless number of men tended to make my exhibitionist sex partner a little hot and bothered, to say the least.

As the shower was heating up, I stood in front of the mirror and once again debated whether I should buy something to cover up the grays, which were slowly taking over the majority from the browns on that slowly receding hairline of mine. My decision, as always, was to wait until they caught up before doing anything that could jeopardize my macho image. If the day ever comes that I do decide to dye the grays, I can always use the excuse that, since I've been told on several occasions that I possess a slight resemblance to Bill Clinton, I was afraid that people would start confusing the two of us.

After stepping out of the shower, I dried myself off and plopped right down on my king-sized bed. I fell asleep before my head hit the pillow but was woken up hours later by you-know-who. She was down there doing her thing, her long brown hair flopping all over the place. Then she came up for air and wrapped her lips and her legs around mine.

I kept my eyes closed from then on. I don't usually, because I'm a voyeur by nature, like most men. But in fantasy, the eyes stay shut and the mind does the viewing and my mind had no problem whatsoever visualizing the voluptuous Lisa Sanchez every step of the way.

CHAPTER 7

As soon as I arrived at my office the next morning, I took the calendar out of my desk drawer. This particular calendar had all of the months of the year on one page. I had penciled in each victim's name, on the day of their murder. I had studied it many times before, too many times, looking for a pattern. I'd counted the days between the murders, divided, added and multiplied all of them, over and over again. You name it, I tried it. Now, with a fourth victim, maybe something would fit into a pattern. But if I was nothing else I was a realist and I wasn't real hopeful.

After driving myself crazy with my useless little calendar game for the better part of an hour, I went upstairs to submit the basics on Lisa Sanchez, to see how she checked out. When I got back to the precinct, after Claude and I grabbed a quick bite at Mickey D's, her file was ready for me.

The criminal section was as clean as a whistle: no arrests, no warrants, no nothing, not even a speeding ticket. It was in the family profile section, on the following page, where I came across a piece of the puzzle that didn't seem to fit. Under *children* it read "one daughter, Claudia Lisa Sanchez, with a date of birth of November 12, 2001. "Unknown" appeared on the line entitled "name of child's father." Just before I had left her apartment, I had asked to use the bathroom in order to give the place a quick looking over. The bedroom door had been left open and I noticed that it only had one bed in it; it was a twin-sized one, so I figured they weren't sharing it. Besides that, there were no toys or games or anything that would have led one to believe that a kid lived there. I looked further down the page in search of a family member who might be looking after the kid. There were none. Both parents were deceased and she had no siblings.

It then struck me that there was a very real possibility that the reason the kid wasn't living with her mother was because she'd been put up for adoption. So I ran back upstairs and had them run a printout of Claudia Sanchez's current address. It showed it as being the very same Flushing, Queens address as her mother's, which caused my adoption hunch to be short-lived, indeed.

The mystique that had already begun to surround my newfound lady of fantasy just took a bit of a growth spurt. All that was undeniable about her was her almost surreal physical beauty. Whether such was a reflection of what lay beneath or a façade for the unsightliness there, I hadn't a clue.

CHAPTER 8

She parked next to the church's rear door and placed the dark black veil over her head.

Upon entering the church, she walked into the confessional booth and locked the door behind her.

Slowly, she knelt down beneath the screen.

"Forgive me Father, for I have sinned."

"How so?"

"I have seen something very terrible take place."

"We all witness terrible events so often these days, do we not?"

"But I have sinned, Father, for what I witnessed was an act against the Lord's Commandments."

"That is an unfortunate part of the world in which we live. We witness the Commandments being broken every day, either firsthand, or else we see it on the news or read about it in newspapers."

"But I did not witness that which was witnessed by others. What I saw, I saw alone. Only my eyes witnessed the horror of this event."

"Would you care to talk more about this, to put your conscience at peace?"

"My conscience will never be at peace, Father, for I witnessed a young child being carried off against her will."

"Did you report such an event to the police?"

"I can't, Father."

"Why is that?"

"Because he who committed this evil act is a messenger of God. To go against him would be a sin."

"Certainly an angel would not commit such an act. What kind of messenger of the Lord could you be speaking of?"

"A messenger who leads God's children in Mass on Sunday mornings and to whom God's children confess their sins."

CHAPTER 9

With his knees resting on the earth below, he held back the branch that obstructed his view.

There they were - the twins, just a stone's throw away.

"I love the odds, mommy."

The thought made him smirk.

He felt real good about this one, two to choose from and only one set of eyes to watch over them. The idea of trying for both at one time was quite appealing but he quickly dismissed it so as not to risk inciting the others. He needed them on his side to complete the act.

Back and forth, they tossed the little pink ball, over and over and over again. Then, it happened! Briana threw the ball over Briane's head.

Up and down it bounced on the black pavement, finally landing in the thick blue spruce in front of him. Quickly, he reached forward and snatched it up.

Briane lifted up the branches of the bush in search of the ball.

"Psst, little girl, it's right here," he whispered.

She looked up at him and smiled, and then reached her arm forward. Just as she was about to grab hold of it, he threw it over the head of her twin sister, Briana, who chased after it as their mother watched.

"Hey, why'd you do that?"

Without any warning, he grabbed hold of her arms and pulled her through the bush to the other side.

In one non-stop motion, he placed his hand firmly over her mouth, balanced her over his shoulder and then took off, without slowing down until he reached his black Honda.

With the young Briane trembling in the passenger seat, he drove on for many miles. Then, just like he'd done in the past, he pulled off the road and slowly proceeded into the woods.

As the sobbing Briane Rodgers lay there with her arms and legs tied to the legs of the table and the noose tightly secured around her neck, she repeated his words, through the sobs and sniffles, as best she could.

When it was all over, he stood there for quite some time, watching her limp body sway back and forth in the stale summer air.

"You have died twice, my child," he screamed at the tiny, lifeless body of Briane Rodgers, "once in the presence of my blood-thirsty eyes and once in the soul of your darling, young twin."

The others giggled in unison.

As he bent down to gather up his belongings, they responded with few, soft pats on the back.

"A job well done," they whispered.

Then, they disappeared.

CHAPTER 10

It was a pleasant surprise to hear the sound of Ken Vecchia's voice as I played back the message that he'd left on my answering machine. Ken was a friend of mine from way back. I hadn't seen or spoken with him since our thirtieth high school reunion, nearly five years prior.

We used to see one another quite often, but that was some years back, when I was still living with my daughter, Jill, and my first wife. We were like family to him back then. "Uncle Kenny" is how Jill used to refer to him, in fact.

Ken was the type of guy who became a priest so he could help people. He'd always been that way - real caring and concerned. He was also one of the most genuine people I've ever known. There were no airs about Ken whatsoever.

After taking Sparky out for a quick walk, I called Father Ken back. We chatted briefly about nothing in particular.

Then he got to the point.

"I need to speak to you, Max."

"I'm all ears, Ken."

"No, I'd like to talk with you in person."

Ken's usual, tranquil voice was starting to sound a little shaky.

"Sure, Ken, no problem. Pick a day and time."

"How's tonight, Max?"

"Tonight's fine, just tell me where and when."

"Mind if we make it your place?"

"My place is fine, Ken."

He arrived at 8:50, ten minutes earlier than he said he would. Thank God for that. I couldn't have taken another ten minutes of driving myself crazy, trying to figure out what was on his mind.

I poured us each a cup of coffee, then had Ken follow me into the living room. I waited until he had sat down on the couch by the front window before I sat down in my easy chair across from him.

Ken took a couple of sips of coffee before he spoke.

"I never in a million years thought I'd be doing this."

20

Then he took a few more sips, probably to stall the process a bit.

"I realize that I should have come to you sooner but my conscience would not allow it. After much soul-searching, however, I decided to call you."

The combination of his apologetic tone and the crackling of his voice left little doubt in my mind that Ken had just delivered the soft jabs that come just before the knockout punch.

"I heard a confession the other morning which disturbs me greatly. I think that it might be connected to those young girls who were so brutally murdered. A woman confessed to me that she witnessed a young girl being carried off against her will. When I asked her why she didn't call the police, she told me that doing so would be a sin because the man was a clergyman, a priest."

Pow! There went the adrenaline shooting through me like a high-speed bullet.

"Did you see the woman who told you this, Ken?"

"No. No I didn't. It was in the confessional booth."

Then I asked what I had to, even though I knew that it would put my amiable childhood buddy on the spot.

"Ken, I need your okay to install a surveillance camera in the booth."

Despite the high degree of regard that I held for Ken, the troubled look on his face didn't faze me one bit. I'd seen too much anguish and despair on the faces of young parents with dead daughters to give a hoot about Ken's moment of inner turmoil.

The telephone started ringing just as Ken was about to say something. When he realized that I wasn't making any attempt to answer it, he began speaking.

"I'm willing to let you have someone watch to see who comes to confession. I'll tell if and when it's that same lady, but I can't do what you asked. It's against the ethics of the Church and priesthood; it would be a sin."

I was about to tell him that a number of priests, who had made the news because of unspeakable things that they had done to young children, should have been worried about such things, and that doing something that might save some little

21

girl's life couldn't be unethical, the way I saw it. But before I had a chance to say anything, I heard the Sarge's voice coming through the answering machine. So I ran to my bedroom to pick up the phone.

"Earl, it's me, I'm here," I yelled.

The recorder turned off.

"Did you hear any of what I was saying, Max?"

"No, nothing."

I could tell by the sound of his voice that I didn't want to, either.

"It's not good news, Max. It happened in the playground of an elementary school in Farmingdale; kid's name was Briane Rodgers, age five."

I wanted to ask him if there were any witnesses this time, but was too damn distressed to even get the words out. So I just hung up.

When my tears finished running their course, I walked back into the living room. Ken read it on my face. My dried-up tears gave it away. I nodded my head to let him know that he'd read it correctly.

Then we both took a few steps forward and grabbed hold of each other.

Ken's whole body was shaking. I felt wetness on my neck, from his tears. I knew that he was feeling a lot of guilt, just like I was. He wept in my arms for quite a while. When he regained his composure, the priest within him stepped aside and Ken Vecchia, the person, spoke.

"Okay Max, you can do it. The surveillance camera, you can do it. These horrific murders have got to stop. They've got to, Max."

CHAPTER 11

The following morning, Claude and I decided to go to the Sterling Diner, down the block from the precinct, to discuss things over breakfast. We both seemed to think more clearly there, probably because their "melt in your mouth" Belgian waffles give us a renewed sense of energy.

After grabbing a couple of copies of *Newsday* on the way in, we sat ourselves down in the unoccupied section of the diner, to the right of the entrance. We held off any conversation until we were done stuffing our faces with Belgian waffles, smothered with pure maple syrup.

"So what do you think about the confession that Ken Vecchia told me about yesterday?"

"Who the heck knows, Max? New York's a mighty big place; there are a lot of crazy people out there."

"There sure are. But it seems a little coincidental, Lisa Sanchez telling me that she dreams that the killer is a priest and some lady in a confessional claiming to see a priest take off with a kid. Wouldn't you agree?"

"Yeah, I would. But like I said, there are a lot of people who have a hard time differentiating reality from imagination. So who knows?"

"I think it would be a good idea if someone kept a tail on Lisa Sanchez for a few days. You agree?"

"We've got to do something, Max. This motherfucker just took down two little girls in less than a week."

"I think you should go it alone, Claude. I don't want to take any chances of her spotting me there."

"Yeah. Good idea."

"Can you start tonight?"

"I've got the girls' chorus recital tonight. I've been promising them for months that I'll be there. So what do you say we make it tomorrow night?"

"Sounds like a plan, Claude. I'll get the okay from Sergeant Bilko, or I should say, I'll relay the message to him that we're doing it."

Sergeant Bilko, a.k.a. Sergeant Earl Monahan, was our head honcho. He has on more than one occasion, expressed to Claude and me the deep sense of trust that he holds for us, which is why he usually has no problem with us calling our own shots.

Claude and I have always felt a great deal of admiration for the Sarge. That is not to say, however, that there aren't times when he can be a first-rate pain in the ass, like most bosses, I guess.

CHAPTER 12

He reached over and turned up his radio, to full volume. *"BRIANE RODGERS IS SURVIVED BY HER PARENTS AND TWIN SISTER, BRIANA."*

Smiling proudly, he turned the radio off and jumped out of bed. He hurried over to the mirror and stood there, staring hard at his reflection. At the top of his lungs, he screamed, *"WE HAVE NOTHING TO FEAR BUT FEAR ITSELF AND, OF COURSE, THE ALMIGHTY HANGMAN!"*

The reflection looked him in the eye and smiled.

"Watch this," he said, as he hopped onto his bed and jumped up and down, trying to jump high enough to bang his head on the ceiling.

"OW!" he shouted, upon accomplishing his feat.

"What's that you say, boys and girls - one more time? Well, the Hangman needs to hear some noise."

"One more time! One more time!"

He cupped his hand behind his ear and shouted, *"I can't hear you!"*

"ONE MORE TIME! ONE MORE TIME!"

He was screaming so loudly that his voice had become hoarse.

"OW," he screamed, in a dry, raspy voice as his head once again slammed into the ceiling.

"How'd you like Uncle Hangman that time, kids? Was that something, or what?"

He jumped and jumped and clapped and clapped, until eventually he fell face down on his bed, exhausted. Moments later, he jumped back up and raised his arms high in the air.

"What a great idea! What a genius the Hangman is!"

He hurried back to the mirror.

"What's that you say, Briana dear? Playtime is over? Is that what I heard? You know something? You're right. Playtime IS over, and do you know what that means? It means that it will have to be beddy-bye time, when you're fast asleep, dreaming of teddies and dollies and poor little sis.

Then he lay back down and stared at the ceiling. *"Beddy*

bye-bye time it will be. Sweet dreams, my child."

CHAPTER 13

Claude began trailing Lisa Sanchez around the clock as we had planned. Doing so was testing his nerves, but good. She hadn't left her apartment, other than to go to work at her housekeeping job at North Shore Hospital each morning. Once there, she didn't leave the hospital's premises until her workday ended at 6 p.m. Claude told me that he'd read more magazine and newspaper articles over the three days that he sat in his car, passing the hours, than he usually cares to read in three months. He even read the editorials, which is definitely not a common practice for Claude because, as he likes to put it, "I don't need others to do my thinking for me."

On the third and final evening, things changed in a hurry. Claude caught sight of Lisa walking out the front door of her apartment building, carrying a gym bag over her shoulder.

She got into her car and slowly pulled away from the curb. Claude did the same.

When he saw her turn right at the stop sign, he assumed that she headed for the Bally's gym, a few blocks down. But as she proceeded past it without slowing down, he realized that he was mistaken.

A while later, Claude picked up his cell phone and called me.

"Hey Max, she's getting onto the Thruway, heading north."

"Wow. She's driven a pretty long way. Wonder where she's going."

"I'll let you know as soon as I do."

"Don't lose her, Claude."

"Don't lose her? How the hell could I lose her, she's driving forty-five in the right lane. I would have driven my kid's motor scooter had I known she drives as fast as a fucking tortoise with no legs."

"All right, calm down Claude. We both know that keeping a tail on someone isn't real exciting police work, but it is real important."

"Yeah, I guess. Oh, by the way, have you heard anything else from your friend, Ken Vecchia?"

"No, nothing yet."

"Okay Max, I'll call you when Little Miss Speed Demon gets off the Thruway, which could be in a day or two at the pace she's going."

CHAPTER 14

I was dozing off in my easy chair when Claude called me back.

"H-e-l-l-o," I said, through a yawn.

"She got off at the West Point exit a little while ago."

"WHAT?"

"Shall I say it in French? Would that help?"

"What the fuck's she doing at West Point?"

"Nothing, I said that she got off at that *exit*. She didn't head in the direction of the academy, though."

"Thank God for that. For a minute there, I thought we had the Federal Government involved in this."

"They've got enough terrorists to hunt down, they don't need this guy on their list right now."

"Well, he is a terrorist."

"You gonna start getting philosophical on me again, Max?"

"The guy's a terrorist, Claude. Why? Because he preys on the innocent and because he's a coward who, I'm sure, is blaming his own ills and inadequacies on others."

"You know, you're starting to actually make sense for once."

"Think about it, Claude. Why do you think those guys flew into the twin towers? Because they were a bunch of brainwashed wimps who had to justify their own inadequacies by murdering innocent people, just like this guy is doing!"

"You're making some real good points, Max, but in the meantime, she just turned into Bear Mountain Park and the road ahead looks to be a bit too winding to be talking and driving at the same time. So I'll speak with you later."

After I hung up the phone, I headed to the kitchen and grabbed a couple of chocolate-covered Entenmann's donuts and a glass of milk. Then I sat down on the living room couch and clicked on the television to watch the news.

Before the news came on, I suffered through some moronic commercial which showed a dozen or so asexual-looking young adults with their backs to the camera, wearing snug tight jeans and nothing on top.

The news commenced, with a camera focusing in on the Rodgers' home.

29

"There is so much despair occupying this residence at 42 Denmar Street in Farmingdale," said the attractive blonde news reporter standing in front of it.

"For Dan and Debra Rodgers and twin sister, Briana, it is an unimaginable nightmare that has come to life."

She went on with her melodramatic bullshit for another minute or two before signing off.

Then, all of sudden, I started to feel a real sense of uneasiness about the newscast I just watched. I couldn't put my finger on why that was.

Then it struck me! Was this piece of dirt gloating over some newscast, while he jotted down the address of the residence where his latest victim's twin sister remains alive?

I sat there, thinking about it as I munched away on my donuts. By the time I had finished devouring donut number two, my feeling of uneasiness had turned into a full-pledged sense of concern.

I tried telling myself over and over that he finds his victims in playgrounds while they're running around having fun, and that he doesn't target any little girl in particular. But I still couldn't convince myself. It kept bothering the living hell out of me.

CHAPTER 15

Claude parked his car at the end of the parking lot opposite to where Lisa Sanchez had just pulled in.

Keeping a safe distance behind, he followed her up the thin, dirt trail, heading towards one of the park's campsites. Upon arriving at the site, he hid behind a cabin which stood directly across from the one that Lisa Sanchez was entering. He waited a few minutes after she walked inside, and then made his way towards the front of the cabin.

Once there, he counted the number of cabins that he saw. There were eight in total, situated in such a way that, together, they formed a large circle. In the center of this circle of cabins, sat a huge campfire, with a dozen, or so, benches surrounding it.

Then he heard something. It was the sound of footsteps coming from outside the cabin which he was hidden beside. So he lay down on the grass and crept to a spot beside the cabin where he was sure that he couldn't be seen.

When all was quiet, he slowly made his way to the front of the cabin one step at a time.

He was caught off guard by what he saw. Gathered about the campfire were women and young girls of grade school age. Dozens of each. There were nuns as well; six of them, dressed in full attire.

He looked around but didn't see her, at first. Then she caught his eye. She was seated on the end of one of the benches with one of the young girls sitting upon her lap.

The very moment that Claude caught a glimpse of the little girl's face, he knew who she was. The resemblance made it a dead giveaway - same pale brown skin, same soothingly attractive features.

One of the nuns then stood on a bench and asked for silence.

"Mothers," she began, "on behalf of my fellow sisters, I'd like to say that we're thrilled that you were able to join us. Obviously, so are your daughters."

She waited for the chatter to fade before continuing.

"As you all know, Father Stanton is away, so please, let's

keep this little secret amongst us girls. Now, if you'd all please have a seat, it's time to light the campfire."

The sister stood beside the campfire, looking around at all the smiling faces.

"In honor of this great country that we're so blessed to be living in, our first song of the evening will be 'God Bless America.'

Next came "America, the Beautiful."

Claude stood there, watching, as they sang song after song.

When the songs had all been sung, he watched as they said goodnight to one another and then walked back to their cabins.

He waited until all was quiet, and then headed down the dirt path to his car in the unpaved parking lot.

CHAPTER 16

Sparky's barks and howls awakened me to the ringing of the doorbell. I glanced over at my alarm clock, it was half past midnight. I grabbed my gun out of the top drawer of my night table and shot out of bed. Then I threw on my bathrobe as I hurried down the hallway, detouring through the kitchen to toss a couple of dog treats to Sparky, to quiet him down.

With my gun drawn and my back against the wall, I stood beside the front door.

"Who is it," I yelled, in my authoritative-sounding police voice.

"It's the three little pigs," I heard Claude shout in a slow, monotone voice, "Let us in before we blow your fucking house down."

I tried not to give him the satisfaction of a grin as I opened the door to let him in.

"What's the matter, you didn't want to use up the minutes on your cell phone? You scared the living shit out of me! Why the hell didn't you call first?"

My partner didn't look like he was in a very apologetic mood. In fact, Claude had the same look on his face that he had when I first told him that Kerri was going to be moving in with me. It was one of those "you've got to be fucking kidding me" types of looks.

"Because I didn't want to wake you," Claude sarcastically replied.

I ignored the comment.

"Get ya some coffee, partner?"

Claude nodded his head, and then followed me into the kitchen.

"Got any cake to go with it," he grunted, as he sat himself down at my kitchen table.

"Cake? I think I can do better than that."

My partner actually let out about a half of a grin when I placed down in front of him a paper plate supporting the weight of two chocolate-covered Entenmann's donuts.

"So what's doing up at Bear Mountain?"

"You wouldn't believe me if I told you."

"Well, tell me anyway."

"She went there to visit her daughter."

"You're kidding!"

"I kid you not. There must have been a couple of dozen mothers there, with their daughters. To top it all off, there were a half dozen nuns there as well."

I sat there, waiting for the punch line.

"I'm going back there tomorrow to check things out with the front office. I'm curious to see the name that the campsite was reserved under."

Well, so much for punch lines.

"I'll take a ride with you. What were they doing up there, anyway?"

"They were sitting around a campfire, singing songs."

"What kind of songs?"

"'God Bless America' 'Battle Hymn of the Republic,' you name it."

"Was it some kind of camp sleep-out?"

"Beats the hell out of me, Max. And speaking of being beat to hell, I better get home before I fall asleep in your kitchen chair. Thanks anyway for the coffee, but I'm too damn tired to even lift up the cup."

I made no mention of the fact that he'd had no such trouble with the donuts.

After Claude slowly stood up, I walked him to the door.

"There's something I want to run by you tomorrow concerning the Briane Rodgers murder. I figured tonight wasn't a real good time, but it's been bugging the shit out of me all night."

"Yeah, tomorrow sounds much better. I'll pick you up at eight, Max."

"Safe home, partner."

CHAPTER 17

His jet-black Honda glided past the modest Cape Cod at 42 Denmar Street in Farmingdale, looking as if it were stuck in slow motion.

"God, I love it. It's so disgustingly typical."

In turn, his most cherished thought came to mind. "It's so utterly fascinating how EVERYONE feels the effects of the Hangman's acts, not just mommy and daddy and sis and friends, but EVERYONE."

When he got to the end of the street, he sat there, debating whether to drive around the block and take another look.

"Ah, what the heck," he muttered.

As he passed by the Rodgers' residence the second time, he envisioned the inside of their modest Cape Cod: two bedrooms at the top of the stairs, one cluttered with dolls and toys, where the twins slept, right across from mommy and daddy's room.

Then a loud voice came blaring out of nowhere,

"LET'S GO PAL, THIS ISN'T A MUSEUM."

He glanced in his rearview mirror. There was a dark blue Ford following him.

"A fucking, undercover cop car, damn it! How idiotic of me to have gone around a second time."

When he came to the end of the block, he turned left this time. Then he took a quick glance in his rearview mirror. The Ford was turning right.

Through his nostrils, he breathed a deep sigh of relief.

CHAPTER 18

On our drive up to Bear Mountain, I called the New York State Police and requested that they have someone meet us at the entrance to the park.

Sure enough, a tall, thin officer was at the front gate waiting to greet us.

"Officer James Quinn," he said, as he extended his right arm through Claude's open window.

"Detectives Max Miller and Claude Greer. Thanks for meeting with us," I said as we shook hands.

"How can I be of assistance to you gentlemen?"

"We'd like to find out the name under which one of the campsites is registered," Claude responded.

"Without anyone else knowing that we're asking, that is," I added.

"Not a problem," the officer said from under his wide-brimmed NY Park Police hat. "Which campsite are you referring to?"

"It's the one where the nuns are staying," Claude answered.

With an apologetic look on his face, Officer Quinn said, "I'm afraid I don't know which one that would be, Detective. I don't recall seeing any nuns here."

"That's probably because they only arrived here last night," Claude said.

"How about if I make you a copy of the reservation list?"

"Good idea," Claude responded.

"Would you guys like to follow me to the park headquarters?"

Although I knew that the odds were pretty remote, I didn't want to take the chance of Lisa Sanchez spotting me there and I figured that trailing a park police jeep was as good a way as any for that to happen.

"Why don't we wait for you at that Dunkin' Donuts that we passed, just down the road from here?" I asked.

Claude and the officer smiled simultaneously, at what I didn't know.

"You had to make it a Dunkin' Donuts, huh, Max?"

"Well, where else are cops supposed to spend their time?" I

asked, joining in on the joke.

"I'll meet you gentlemen there as soon as possible," Officer Quinn said as he hopped aboard his jeep.

After we watched him pull away, Claude drove off to the Dunkin' Donuts down the road. When we arrived there, I ordered a couple of cups of coffee and jelly donuts and then brought them outside to our air-conditioned car.

"What's on the inside?" Claude asked, as he took his donut out of the bag.

"What are you, kidding me? Like you've never seen the inside of a fucking Dunkin' Donuts?"

"No, you asshole, I mean what's inside the donut."

"Why, like you're not gonna eat it no matter what it is?"

"Good point," he said with a smile, before taking a giant mouthful.

"Hey Claude, you do know that Briane Rodgers had a twin sister, right?"

Claude wiped the white sugar off his lips before responding.

"Of course I do. Why?"

"Well, I've got a funny feeling that he's going to try going after her."

"What makes you think that?"

"I was watching the news last night and they were showing the house she lives in. I think this psychotic fuck is watching it too. He's probably gloating over it like a fucking gorilla does over a banana."

"But we've got undercover there already."

"I know that we do. But with the way that this prick has been eluding the pants off of us, I don't think that's going to be enough."

"Then what do you suggest?"

"I think we might need someone on the inside, 24-7."

"You're asking a lot, Max. The last thing that we want to do is to scare the crap out of any of the victims' parents. They're going through enough heartache as it is. And besides that, I don't think that I agree with you, anyway. This guy's a fucking loaded gun. I don't think he does a lot of planning ahead. He just takes off with whichever little girl is his easiest target at the time."

37

"I know what you're saying, Claude. But I've just got this funny feeling, especially since the twin was at that playground when he took off with...."

"Hey, here he is," Claude said as Officer Quinn pulled into the spot next to us.

Claude rolled down his window.

"Here you go, Detective," Quinn said, handing Claude a white, sealed envelope.

"Much obliged, Officer," Claude said as he reached up to shake his hand.

I leaned over to do the same.

"Let us know if there are any goings-on up here that you think we should know about," I said, as I handed him my card.

"I sure will, Detective. And if you need anything else, just give me a call."

As the amiable officer pulled away, Claude ripped open the envelope and began searching up and down the list like a madman. He reminded me of a high school kid looking to see if he made the cut on the football team.

"There it is, Max."

Claude leaned over to show me his find: The Thomas Stanton School, Jackson Heights, NY.

"Do you really think that it's a *school,* Claude? It's the middle of the summer and it sure didn't sound like some run-of-the-mill summer school class that you witnessed taking place there last night."

"It's the name, Thomas Stanton. The nun said something to the effect of "let's make sure Father Stanton doesn't find out about this."

I looked Claude in the eye.

"Are you sure?"

"I'm fucking positive."

"I wonder why the big secret."

"Who knows, maybe he's just one of those types who prefers it when everyone else is as miserable as he is. You know the type."

"Well, if that happens to be the case partner, then I reckon that it would be fair for me to say that we should find out a little more about the guy."

38

"I reckon so," Claude replied.

CHAPTER 19

As of two weeks ago, we hadn't a trace of a clue. Now we had a couple of traces. The only problem was that they could wind up leading us straight down a dead-end path. My gut feeling, though, was that we were heading in the right direction. Lately, those gut feelings of mine had more often than not turned out to be pretty much on target.

Last winter, for example, I was assigned to a case in which some guy put a hole in the head of this seventeen-year-old kid, who he said he caught breaking into his house. It appeared to be an open-and-shut case, to everyone but me, that is. Something led me to believe that he was lying through his teeth. Nothing in particular, just that feeling in my gut.

Sure enough, it turned out that the guy was having sexual encounters with the kid after his wife would go to bed. On one particular night, he asked the kid to perform some unmentionable endeavors that the kid wanted no part of. A heated argument ensued, during which the kid got dressed and informed him that he was going home to reveal their relationship to his foster parents.

A bullet in the back of the kid's head on the way out the door put an end to that idea.

There were quite a few differences between this case and that one, though, the biggest one being that the longer this one took to solve, the greater the chance that more innocent little girls would be whisked away into the woods to die a slow, tortuous death at the hands of some psychopathic loser. This brought to mind another one of those gut feelings of mine: If I'm the one that catches him and if there's no one nearby when I do, I'm going to kill him right then and there, with my bare hands. Hopefully I'm wrong, though, because I'd rather he be sent to the slammer, where he'll be given a taste of his own medicine many times over. If he had any idea what that would be like, he'd be on his hands and knees begging me to kill him right then and there.

As we pulled into one of the empty spaces in the precinct's parking lot, I realized that other than a few choice words which Claude directed at an occasional driver along the way, neither

40

of us had said a word during our long drive back to the precinct. This meant that I wasn't the only one lost in thought for the past hour.

"What's the matter, cat got your tongue?" I asked as we walked towards the rear entrance of the precinct.

Claude didn't respond. I glanced over at him; he didn't glance back.

A few moments later, he turned to me and said, "I keep getting these flashes of Pam and Tamara hanging from some tree with a noose around their necks. It's like a fucking living nightmare."

I stopped dead in tracks, which caused Claude to stop as well.

"Maybe you should consider taking yourself off the case, Claude. Sounds as though this one's starting to feel a bit too close to home, understandably so."

He didn't reply at first. But when we got to the top of the ramp, by the rear entrance, he turned to me and said, "That's all the more reason for me to stay on I want the opportunity to rip him apart with my bare hands."

Without saying a word, I planted my teeth firmly upon my lower lip and then turned around to open the rear door of the precinct.

CHAPTER 20

The tips of his fingers were begging for his mercy. Reluctantly, he unraveled the string that was strangling off their flow of fresh blood and threw it down, disgusted with himself for giving in. Then he pulled off the glove, one finger at a time, and let it fall to the ground. His middle fingers had turned a dark shade of red at their tips, his pinkie an even darker shade, with a bluish tint, making it appear as though all life had been drained from it. He resisted the urge to rub them, to help soothe their pain, as much for the strict self-discipline required as for his impeccable ability to keep his fingerprints off of the places where others might want them to be. After allowing his beleaguered hand the luxury of a few minutes of breathing time, he crouched down to retrieve the glove. While remaining crouched, he carefully tugged it back on and then wrapped the string around it, a tad less tightly than before.

Well hidden beside the cabin, he peeked over at the girls sitting quietly around the campfire. There were so many of them that he thought it a shame that he must have only one.

"Three's a crowd," a voice sharply snapped at him.

"With the mommies now gone, it's almost too damn easy," he responded, in jest.

The decision as to which one it would be was an easy one.

"The redhead will be dead before her next meal is fed."

He had never had a redhead before.

Close to an hour passed before the girls headed back to their cabins to call it a night.

"What a lucky man that Hangman is," he whispered as the red-haired girl walked into the very same cabin which he was hidden behind.

He looked at his watch. It was 9:48, two hours was the least he had figured it would take until she and her bunkmates were sound asleep.

To play it safe, he waited until midnight, at which time he pulled the ski mask out of his back pocket and placed it over his head. Then he crept, as slowly as his legs would allow, to the front of the cabin and up the few steep steps. Slowly, he pulled open the screen door, just wide enough for his body to squeeze

42

through.

Once inside, he stood as still as a statue in the foyer area. He listened hard to make certain that all was quiet. Then he slowly tiptoed into the bedroom.

He looked around at the four bunk beds, one against each of the walls. Then he crept along the wall towards the bunk bed to his left, and peeked to check the faces - first the top and then the bottom.

Then he moved on to the next.

There she was, on the top bed, sound asleep!

Slowly, he unwound the string from his hand.

Much to his delight, her pillow had elevated her head just enough to make the task of threading the string, many times around her neck a much easier one than expected.

"Sweet dreams, my child," he whispered.

Then he pulled tight the string with so much force that the little red-haired girl never got a chance to wake up.

Slowly, he unwound the string from around her neck.

He glanced around the room. Then he lifted her up and carried her outside, to the back of the cabin. After laying her body down on the grass, he debated what to do next.

He decided to bypass the ceremony, since the participant would not be an unwilling one. Instead, he picked her up, slipped her head through the hanging noose and tightened it around her neck.

Quickly, he released her from his grip.

He stood there for a while, admiring his accomplishment.

Then he turned and crept through the woods to the dirt path, where he strolled along, quite nonchalantly, occasionally kicking up some dirt.

The Hangman was feeling quite blasé over this latest act.

"A mere training session for the twin," he boasted.

The others giggled loudly at his cockiness, at the confidence that he once so lacked.

43

CHAPTER 21

The Thomas Stanton School turned out to be legit. The report that I had requested called it an all-expenses-paid private boarding school for underprivileged girls of Catholic descent. It was registered with and certified by the State of New York. It was described as "a highly competitive learning institution, with an enrollment of only thirty-two students, all possessing exceptionally high levels of intelligence." Within the report was a list of the students' names, shown in alphabetical order. Towards the bottom of the list appeared the name Claudia Sanchez. Her home address was the same as Lisa Sanchez's; same apartment number as well.

Thus it appeared more likely than ever that Lisa Sanchez was nothing more than some devoutly religious parent who was having dreams containing religious connotations, which had nothing whatsoever to do with the case at hand. As for Thomas Stanton, it was verified that the deposit given for the campsite was made via a check showing the school as the payer - something he might have taken exception to.

Such theories were, of course, nothing more than heightened speculation, which my partner had already begun to praise as gospel. I, on the other hand, was sticking by that feeling in my gut: There was more to it than met the eye.

The phone call which I received that morning confirmed my suspicions once and for all.

"Detective Miller, it's Officer Quinn of the Bear Mountain State Police. This morning, we found the body of a young girl. It was hanging from a tree at the same campsite that you and Detective Greer were inquiring about. The details are still somewhat sketchy. We do know, however, that she was one of the girls who'd been staying at that site. What we don't know as of yet is whether she had strayed from the site or if she'd been abducted while she was sleeping. I'll be sure to keep you informed of any further findings that we come across."

Without saying goodbye, I hung up the phone, yanked its cord from the wall and flung it across the room into the pale-green wall across from me.

Fully reclined in my chair, I sat there for quite some time, totally absorbed in thought.

Then, out of nowhere, Claude came barreling into my office with the grace of Frankenstein's monster performing a ballet solo.

Caught off guard, I grabbed hold of my desk to retain my balance.

"Quinn just tried calling you again. What the fuck is wrong with your phone?

Then he spotted it sitting on the floor, but paid it no mind. Instead, he walked over to the front of my desk and leaned way over it. He stared straight at me. He looked real wired, like an evangelist on a sugar high.

"They have a witness," he cried out in jubilation. "One of the kids saw the guy in action last night!"

CHAPTER 22

We made the trip back up to Bear Mountain with the siren off, so as not to draw attention to ourselves. We wanted to be as inconspicuous as possible. The last thing that we needed was the press getting ahold of this before we wanted them to.

By the time that we at arrived the campsite, however, it was already packed with New York State Troopers and Rockland County Police Officers. But much to our delight, there were no news vans in sight. We glanced around the place, looking for Officer Quinn, but couldn't spot him among the huge gathering of police officers. So we introduced ourselves to the first officer that we came across. He, in turn, introduced us to the two New York State detectives who had spoken with the witness.

The first bit of information that they relayed to us took me by surprise. It appeared as though the victim had been strangled to death before the noose was put around her neck. It's highly unusual for a killer such as this to start changing techniques in midstream. The thought did cross my mind that maybe this one was unrelated to the others. But I knew that the odds of that being the case were much closer to none than slim. If the victim had been shot or stabbed to death, then the likelihood of that being true would have increased dramatically. But this guy had a thing for strangulation, and strangulation was the cause of death.

What the troopers had to say next was quite disheartening, to say the least. As it turned out, the guy was wearing a ski mask to cover his face. Add that to the fact that they went on to say that it was too dark inside the cabin for the witness to make out what he was wearing on the rest of his body, and that gave you two extremely frustrated Nassau County homicide detectives.

To top it all off, we were told that the witness' description of the suspect's height was, in a word, "big." That part didn't surprise me, though, because most kids her age lack the capacity to make certain judgments, the height and age of an adult being two of them. So what we had was a young girl who saw a "big" person wearing a ski mask, not exactly a case-breaking identification by our one and only witness.

46

When they informed us that the campsite had been evacuated a few hours earlier, we thanked them for their time and headed back down the dirt path to our car.

A news van was pulling into the park just as we were pulling out. Claude, being no lover of the media and not exactly in what would be described as the best of moods, started yelling, "It was the man in the ski mask, with a rope in the woods, you no-good bloodsucking leeches!"

So much for our concern over media leaks.

"Where do we go from here?" Claude asked, as we headed back to the Thruway.

"There are two places that I can think of. One is the Thomas Stanton School. The other is Lisa Sanchez's apartment. I'd like to hear what she has to say now."

"What are you going to do, shine bright lights in her eyes to get her to talk, like they did in those World War II movies?"

"You're a real fucking comedian, Claude. Actually, I want to ask her something that I haven't given a lot of thought to. Until now, that is."

"What's that, her bra size?"

"You must not have heard me correctly. I said something that I haven't given a lot of thought to."

Claude glanced over at me and smiled.

"It's something she shouldn't be afraid to answer, unless she's got some reason for wanting to hide it from me."

"All right, stop with the bullshit. Let's hear the million dollar question, already."

"Who's the father of her kid and where is he now?"

"Hey Max, you know as well as I, that the report said that it's unknown who the kid's father is. What part of that are you unable to comprehend?"

"Let me ask you something Claude, from what you saw of her lifestyle, do you really think she sleeps around like that?"

"At the present time? No. But the present isn't always a very good indicator of what someone was like in the past. Believe it or not, Max, some people actually grow up as they get older."

I chose to ignore that little slap in my face.

"It's an awfully strange coincidence that the murder occurred

47

at the same place that she and her daughter were staying, don't you think?" I asked.

"It sure the hell is. But I say that we stop by the school first, so that we can talk to the witness while it's still fresh in her mind. Maybe there's something she left out."

"Yeah, that sounds like a plan, partner."

CHAPTER 23

After getting off the Grand Central Parkway, Claude turned onto Roosevelt Avenue, the main boulevard that runs through Jackson Heights, which is the section of Queens where the Thomas Stanton School is located. It's way outside the boundaries of my Nassau County jurisdiction. But I knew quite well that Roosevelt Avenue had a reputation for being a place where it's no more difficult to purchase an ounce of pot or a few grams of cocaine than a pack of cigarettes or a six-pack of beer.

Although the school was located a mere dozen or so blocks from Roosevelt Avenue, it would not be considered to be within the same neighborhood. Nor for that matter did it seem as though the two places belonged in the same universe. The well-kept three-story apartment building that housed the school looked like the kind of place where the Sleeping Beauty would be waiting for her Prince Charming to arrive. It had that storybook air about it, that look of perfection only found in such fictional places. The gray colored bricks making up its exterior looked as though some computerized robotic arm had placed them there, with unparalleled precision.

There were no signs or plaques on the outside of the building indicating that a boarding school lay within. That struck me as being a bit odd at first. But then I just shrugged it off to someone being wise enough to not want to broadcast the whereabouts of a place that housed young girls.

When we got to the entrance of the building, I shouted "Police" into the intercom in response to the voice on the other end asking who it was that was requesting entry. Then, as the voice requested, I held my badge in front of the surveillance camera.

Claude pulled open the door at the sound of the buzzer.

The lobby was huge, taking up the entire first floor of the building. It was sparsely decorated, with a few cushioned chairs and small coffee tables scattered about. Other than a small group of paintings nestled together in the far right corner, the walls were bare. Their color made me think that whoever it was that painted the walls of the precinct had a few cans of that ugly pale green paint left over and decided to use them on the walls of the lobby that we were standing in.

When we were done looking around, we walked over to the elevator at the other end of the lobby. It was one of those old, outdated kinds with two doors, an outer one that had to be pulled open and an inner one that opened automatically.

After we stepped inside, I stood there trying to decide which of the two buttons to push, the one that said "Offices and Dormitories" or the one above it that read "Classrooms".

I looked over at Claude. He shrugged his shoulders. So, I pushed in the bottom one, figuring that in a school of that size it didn't make a whole heck of a difference.

We stepped out of the elevator and into a long hallway with a staircase running smack through the middle of it. There were eight or nine rooms surrounding the staircase. We took a few steps past it and saw that one of the doors had the words "Main Office" written upon it. So we gave it a try.

The nun who opened the door introduced herself as Sister Rosemary. Claude later informed me that she was the one who had been running the show at Bear Mountain. After she let us in, we asked to speak with Father Stanton. She informed us that he was overseas, in Germany, visiting family. She told us that he goes there about this same time every year, for about a month.

So Claude asked permission to speak with LeAnn Danielle, the little girl who had witnessed the murder.

"She wanted to go home, to be with her parents," Sister Rosemary said, holding back tears. "She was terribly frightened."

"She's a very brave little girl," I softly replied.

"I'm surprised Father Stanton didn't want to take the trip up to the country with his students," Claude said.

"I chose not to tell Father Stanton that we were going there," she said as she sat down on the edge of the desk. "I didn't think it would meet with his approval."

She said it real matter-of-factly, as if she had already prepared herself to face the consequences of her decision.

"Does he know about Tracy's murder?" I asked in a very gentle tone that a shrink would perhaps use with an overly sensitive patient.

I hit a nerve with that one, however. Sister Rosemary put her head down and started sobbing pretty heavily. I wanted to walk over and hug her, to comfort her, but I didn't think it would be appropriate, with her being a nun and all. So instead, I walked over and handed her the box of tissues that was sitting on the desk.

When she finished drying her eyes, she looked up at me and said, "He never leaves me with a phone number or address of where he's staying, so I have no way of notifying him."

I nonchalantly glanced over at Claude. He returned my glance. We both thought that it sounded a bit unusual for someone in his position not to leave a phone number where he could be reached.

Then I asked if it would be all right if we had a word with Claudia Sanchez. "Why Claudia?" she asked.

"Well," I said, quite dishonestly, "her mother is a friend of mine."

She stood up and said, "I'll ask her to come down."

She walked over to the intercom but stopped dead in her tracks just as she was about to talk into it. Then she turned to look at me and said, "My goodness, it almost slipped my mind, completely. Mrs. Sanchez drove back to the campsite yesterday, in the early evening. She told me that she needed to take Claudia home for a couple of days."

"Did she say why?"

She stood there thinking for a moment and said, "No, she didn't, but I'm sure it was for something very important, considering that she came all the way back to get her. Mrs. Sanchez and the other mothers had left in the early afternoon, right after lunch. I must have been so preoccupied with organizing the activities for the girls that I hadn't even thought to ask her why she came all the way back to get Claudia."

Seeing that Sister Rosemary was becoming more and more upset, I said, "You've been through a terrible tragedy, Sister Rosemary. Please don't let yourself get upset over something like this. Whatever her reason was for picking up Claudia is of little importance right now."

I was lying through my teeth when I said that, in order to

console the kind, elderly nun. In truth, the question of why Lisa Sanchez came back to get Claudia just hours before the murder sure wasn't going to go unasked for a heck of a lot longer.

CHAPTER 24

We thanked Sister Rosemary for her time and hurried down the stairs to the lobby. From there, we did a slow trot to the front door and picked up the pace a bit when we got outside.

Lisa Sanchez's apartment was about a twenty-five minute ride from the school. Claude made it there in fifteen at the most. He parked in front of a fire hydrant by the main entrance of the building. I tossed the "Police Business" sign on top of the dashboard, in plain view of any NYPD officer who might happen by.

The front door of the building was locked.

I chose not to press the intercom button of her apartment, so as not to give her any advance notice of our arrival. Instead, I rammed my shoulder full force into the front door of the building and *voila'*, the door flew open.

Then, I led the way to the staircase and up the four flights of stairs. When we got to her apartment, I rang the doorbell about four or five times, nonstop. When I heard the sound of the doorknob turning from inside the apartment, I immediately realized that the door wasn't double-locked because there was no sound of locks being turned, like there was the first time that I was there.

When the door opened, a man of average height and weight stood before us. His complexion was the slightest shade of brown. Claude took his badge out of his shirt pocket and shoved it right in front of the guy's face.

"Where is she?" Claude demanded as we entered the apartment.

The man very calmly replied, "If you'd tell me exactly who *she* is, I'd be more than happy to try and answer your question, Officer."

"Who the hell do you think? The lady who lives here, Lisa Sanchez," Claude hastily replied.

"Well, I'm trying to figure that one out myself. As far as I can tell, it looks as though she's moved out."

Claude and I looked at one another in shock. We were probably no less taken aback than we would have been had friends and family popped out of the closets and yelled

"Surprise!"

"Who are *you*?" I asked.

"My name's Jackson Tyler, I'm the super of this building."

"What makes you think that she's moved?"

"Well, it looks like all of her belongings are gone. I've been checking out the water pressure in all of the apartments because we've been having a lot of problems with it recently. I'd left several messages on Mrs. Sanchez's answering machine over the past few days, so that I could gain access into her apartment. She didn't return my calls, so I figured that I'd pay a visit, to make sure that everything was okay."

"How come all of her furniture's still here?" Claude asked, as he walked around, casing the place.

"It's not hers. The place came furnished."

I walked over and sat down on one of the chairs in the small kitchenette area and asked the super to grab the chair across from me. As soon as he was seated, I asked, "What can you tell me about the people that she hung out with?"

"Not a thing. Whenever I saw her, which wasn't very often at all, she was alone."

"You've never seen her with a male companion?"

"No, I haven't. Maybe someone else around here has, but not me."

"Did you ever see a young girl, about seven or eight years old, with her?

The super sat there, thinking, for a minute or so. Then, he said, "Like I said, I really don't remember having ever seen her with anyone."

"How long did she live here?"

"A couple years, I'd say."

Then, all of a sudden, I heard Claude shout, "Hey Max, come here for a minute."

I stood up from the table and hurried over to the bedroom.

"What do you think of this," he asked as he pointed at the banged-in bottom part of the bedroom door.

"Well, I'm pretty darn sure that it wasn't like that last week when I was here. The door was open but I think that I would have noticed something like that. In fact, I know that I would have. That's not exactly a tiny little dent."

"She left here in such a hurry that she might have banged something against it on her way out," Claude said.

"May-BE," I replied, with an obvious touch of skepticism in my voice.

I examined the damaged door for a few moments longer and then stepped inside the bedroom and took a quick look around. Then I walked out of the room and headed towards the front door of the apartment. Claude and the super followed me down the stairs to the lobby.

When we got to the front door of the building, Claude stopped and turned to shake the super's hand. As I took my turn, I said, "Thanks for your time."

"My pleasure, Officer," the amiable young man replied.

As I turned to follow Claude out the door, I realized that I had neglected to give the super my card. So I did an about-face, pulled a card out of wallet and handed it him.

"Give me a buzz if you hear anything," I said.

The super glanced down at my card and said, "You know something, Detective Miller? If I were asked to pick a tenant that was in trouble with the law, I think that she'd be the very last one on my list. That's the God's honest truth."

I nodded my head and then turned around and grabbed hold of the bar on the glass door that Claude had just let go of, so as not to let it close in my face.

CHAPTER 25

If it pours when it rains, as some philosophical genius once said, then I guess it would be fitting of me to say that when we arrived back at the precinct, the monsoon kicked in. There was a message awaiting me saying that Ken Vecchia had called yesterday at 10:33 a.m., which was right after Claude and I had left for Bear Mountain.

I called him back immediately.

What he had to say sounded almost too good to be true. That same woman had come back to his confessional, and he had it on videotape.

"Okay, Ken, stay right there. Please. We're coming right over."

I ran downstairs to the cafeteria, where I found Claude standing around, stuffing his face.

"Let's go!" I yelled, while still in motion. "We're going to church. The lady came back to pay another visit to Ken Vecchia."

When we got to the car, I jumped into the driver's seat and flicked on the siren.

I made it to the parkway in no time flat and then quickly cut all the way over to the left lane. Nobody's more of a raving lunatic behind the wheel when he has to be than yours truly. Well, except for Claude, that is.

"Move over, this is a police emergency!" I shouted into the megaphone at anyone who dared get in my way.

One driver didn't adhere to my command, probably because her age didn't allow her to hear what I was saying, so I drove up onto the shoulder between the guard rail and the lady's car and cut right in front of her. Then I took a quick glance in my rear view mirror. The old lady was cruising along, totally unaware that she was almost run off the road by an unmarked police car.

There were no parking spots to be found near the church, so I hopped the car onto the curb and parked on the sidewalk, right in front of the place.

We ran to the entrance as if we were competing for Olympic gold medals and stopped dead in our tracks when we got inside.

"Can I help you?" a guy in a custodian's uniform asked.

"Father Vecchia," I replied.

He pointed down the hallway to the right of us and said, "Last door on your left."

So off we went.

Ken was sitting at his desk, reading something. He stood up when we walked into the room. I introduced him to Claude, who responded with a courteous, "It's a pleasure to meet you, Father Vecchia. Max has spoken a great deal about you over the years."

"All good, I hope."

"I think "good" would be quite an understatement, *Uncle Kenny.*"

Ken's face lit up like it did when Jill used to call him that, way back when. He'd always been very fond of Jill, and she of him.

He asked us to follow him down the hallway and into an office, where a television monitor sat atop the only desk in the room.

I sat down behind the desk.

"Have you looked at it, yet, Ken?" I asked.

"Nope. That's your department, Max."

So, with Ken standing over my left shoulder, and Claude my right, I hit the play button.

"That's her," Ken said upon hearing her voice.

So I rewound it, and then played it back.

"Damn!" I yelled.

I looked up at Ken in hopes that the woman on the screen might somehow look familiar, despite the fact that a black veil was concealing her identity.

He shook his head.

"Damn!" I yelled, pounding my fist down on the desk.

"I wonder how she knew about the camera," Claude said.

"Chances are she didn't," I replied. "She probably didn't want to be seen by anyone, camera or no camera."

I played it back for Ken a few more times, to no avail.

"Did she at least have anything new to report, Ken?"

"No, not really, Max. She basically reiterated what she had

57

told me the first time. It's apparently not sitting very well on her conscience."

On our ride back to the precinct, Claude took over the wheel at my request. I wanted to spend the time sorting through the events of the nonstop roller coaster ride that we'd been on since the call from Officer Quinn came in that morning.

Instead, I started thinking about, of all things, Bazooka bubble gum. Well, not the gum itself, but rather the tiny Bazooka Joe comic strip that came with it. As a kid, I would save up those comics in hopes of one day having saved enough to get a free pair of those x-ray glasses that they claimed could see through anything. To a young lad like myself that meant seeing right through girls' dresses and their various other garments. But as a grownup, I needed them to see through a veil covering the face of a woman too frightened to come forward unhidden. And, of far greater urgency, to see beneath a ski mask and expose the identity of a sadistic coward who preys on those too weak and vulnerable to defend themselves.

Then I started to wonder what it would be like if those x-ray glasses were so very powerful that they could see right inside the guy's mind, enabling me to see the rage that must surely lay within, and how it came about. I quickly decided, however, that rather than waste my time with such matters, I'd simply take them off and toss them in the nearest waste receptacle. The bottom line was that six little girls were dead, no matter what the reason.

Claude headed inside the station house when we arrived back at the precinct. I, on the other hand, chose to head straight home, having had my bubble burst enough times for one day.

CHAPTER 26

Upon awakening the next morning, I pushed in the "off" button of my alarm clock with a bit more force than usual. It wasn't just the sound of that sudden call to face another day in the working world that I was tuning out. It was also the sound of some guy named Axl Rose, attempting his own deafening rendition of Dylan's "Knockin' on Heaven's Door."

After catching a quick glimpse of Kerri's exposed derriere, I forced myself out of bed before temptation caused me to precipitate the resumption of our under-the-sheets activities from a few hours earlier.

Usually I do a little exercising upon arising in the morning. But on this morning, I headed straight to the kitchen and turned on the percolator.

With my mug of coffee in hand, I sat down in my easy chair. Now that yesterday was history, I was overly anxious to start digesting its events.

With my mind much clearer than it was the previous day, I immediately focused on the fact that Claude had observed Lisa Sanchez leave her apartment for Bear Mountain, carrying a gym bag, which must have contained her change of clothes for the next day. Although she could have had the remainder of her belongings all packed up and waiting for her at that time, the likelihood was far greater that she did the rest of her packing after she left Bear Mountain the first time.

If such assumption was, in fact, correct, then the feeling in my gut, aided by a generous dose of common sense, was that she must have seen or heard someone or something that caused her to suddenly pack up and leave with her daughter.

The question still remained: Was it during her stay at Bear Mountain that this occurred or was it sometime after she left there the first time?

Then, I realized something. It couldn't have been Lisa Sanchez who visited Ken Vecchia's confessional two days ago. Sister Rosemary had told us that all the mothers, Lisa Sanchez included, had made their departure from Bear Mountain in the early afternoon. The lady who gave confession, however, arrived at the church at 10:08 a.m., according to the time on the videotape. Plus, Ken's phone call to me came in at 10:33 a.m., as was documented by the precinct's switchboard operator, which was rock-solid proof of the a.m. time.

So the answering of one question led to more difficult ones. If it wasn't Lisa Sanchez who gave that confession to Ken yesterday, then who could it have been? And, was it Lisa Sanchez who gave confession the first time?

Up until this point, I was pretty darn certain that Lisa was the mystery woman whom Ken had been telling me about when he came to my home that day. But now my gut was telling me, in no uncertain terms, that there was only one lady giving confession to Ken Vecchia. Since the facts now ruled out Lisa Sanchez, not even my trusty old gut could fathom a guess as to who it could possibly be.

A very disturbing thought then found its way into my mind. If Lisa Sanchez did have foresight into the murder, then why didn't she do something to prevent it from happening? Was she too overcome with fear to do so, or, perhaps, too ridden with evil to want to? There also remained the possibility, of course, that she didn't know for certain whether or not it was going to happen.

A lot of questions and so very few answers.

As I was heading to the kitchen to pour myself another cup of coffee, I realized that there was one loose end that we'd have tied up before the day was through. If Father Thomas Stanton did, in fact, go to Germany, as he had told Sister Rosemary, then he sure couldn't have gotten there by flapping his arms up and down.

Airlines keep impeccable records these days.

CHAPTER 27

On this morning, like so many others, he lay in bed before arising for the day, staring straight into the ceiling.

He would see himself, a boy of barely six years of age, aware that his mother had received a call from the school nurse informing her that he'd had an accident, "an embarrassing kind that children his age sometimes have." His mother would hurry to the school to bring his change of clothing. When he arrived home, he'd lay down on his bed with his eyes glued to the television set. He'd pay no attention to what was taking place on the screen, however, being too preoccupied with his impending fate.

"Please God, don't let him find out. Please God. Please."

Most days his stepfather would arrive home happy and cheerful, and he would shout up to him, "How's my little boy doing?" or "How was school today, son?"

The days that he came home unhappy and belligerent were the days that the little boy would hear nothing but the sound of footsteps slowly making their way towards his bedroom.

As his stepfather approached him on this particular day, his unspoken words of prayer became more desperate than ever before.

"Please God, I beg of you. Please, I'll be good, I promise I will. I beg of you, God, please, please, please...."

"I understand you had a little accident in school today, son."

His stepfather lifted him off the bed by his shirt collar, his knuckles grinding into the young lad's chest.

"I couldn't help it, daddy."

"Little sissy boy couldn't help it? What are you crying about, you feeble-minded little sissy?"

"Please, God, don't let him do it. Make him stop, please, please."

His stepfather put him down on the ground.

"You know what to do now, son."

The little boy pulled down his trousers and underwear, then took off one of his shoes and removed its shoelace. He handed the shoelace to his stepfather, who proceeded to bend down and tie it around the boy's genitals.

"Ow! No, daddy, please! No, daddy!"

He tightened the lace even tighter than the last time.

"I thought you would have learned your lesson the first time. Now pick up your god damn pants."

The pain had gone past the point of excruciating by bedtime, when his stepfather barged into his bedroom and cut off the lace with a large scissors.

His genitals had turned a dark, almost purplish color. They were so sore and swollen that he wished he could have removed them, in order to make the hurt go away.

"Next time we'll see if you can't control yourself, you little sissy."

Then his stepfather flicked off the light and slammed the door behind him, leaving the little boy alone in the dark with his pain and his fear, and his unanswered prayers.

CHAPTER 28

"So where does that leave us now?" Claude asked as he placed the sheet of paper back down on my desk.

"At this point, I'd have to say straight up the mouth of the Mississippi without a paddle."

The sheet of paper that Claude had just finished scrutinizing was the passenger list of the prior month's flights from J.F.K. to Munich, Frankfurt and Berlin, Germany. To the astonishment of both my partner and myself, listed in seat 27C of an American Airlines flight to Frankfurt was the name Thomas Stanton.

"So what do you suggest we do now?" Claude asked.

"Follow me," I said.

I led the way down the hallway to Captain Monahan's office.

Once seated, I got right to the point.

"I think it's time to bring the media on board."

Claude and Earl looked at me as if a third eye had just made its appearance in the middle of my forehead. Understandably so, of course, since I, like my partner, was not exactly known to be a lover of the media.

"What for?" Earl asked.

"Well, Son of Sam, for one started communicating through the media."

"That's exactly right, Max. He started communicating when he was ready to."

"Earl, let me ask you a question. At this point in this god-damned investigation, what the hell have we got to lose?"

"What have we got to gain, Max?"

"What the hell do you think? Maybe it'll open the lines of communication. They're closed shut right now. We're on the defensive, one hundred percent. Why not at least attempt to do something about that? What's it going take until we start, another little girl's asphyxiation?"

I got my point across with that one. The frown on Earl's face was a sure sign of that.

"I'll tell you what, Max. How about if you and I sit down with Penny Forrester and get her views on the subject."

I didn't have to give it a second's thought.

"That's fair enough, Earl."

Penny Forrester was a well-known professor of psychiatry at the University at Stony Brook, out in Suffolk County. Although I'd never met the woman, I knew that she'd given guidance on a number of police matters. Nothing of this magnitude, however.

At that point, I was more than willing to get some feedback from someone whose expertise lay in the area of psychopathic human behavior. In fact, I was kind of looking forward to it. Like it or not, I was starting to realize that it may take more than a sharp police mind to nab this demented son of a bitch.

CHAPTER 29

Dr. Forrester's office was nestled in the far left corner of a long row of attached medical suites, in the heart of the quaint waterfront town of Port Jefferson.

Port Jeff, as it is commonly referred to by us Long Islanders, is located a couple of miles east of the University at Stony Brook, where the noted psychiatrist teaches.

Earl opened the outside door to her suite, which led us directly into her waiting room. We sat down on opposite ends of the large leather sofa, across from the entrance. Earl reached over to grab a magazine. I, on the other hand, started eyeballing the pictures on the walls. Each one was of some serene setting, the largest being a beach scene featuring a brilliant sunset glaring beyond the horizon. Its calming effect seemed to radiate throughout the room. Just as the doctor had ordered, I'm sure.

When Dr. Forrester walked into the waiting room a couple of minutes later, I was a little taken aback because she was more attractive than I might have imagined - quite a bit more. The doctor's age was tough to say for certain, but I figured forty or thereabouts was a pretty good guess.

After she and Earl exchanged pleasantries, I took the liberty of beating Earl to the punch by introducing myself. When she turned to look at me, I couldn't help but notice how nicely her sparkling green eyes contrasted with her shoulder-length, jet-black hair.

When we stepped inside her office, the first thing to catch my eye was the big black leather chair in the middle of the room, because it was the exact replica of my easy chair.

I was hoping that Earl wouldn't go for it, which he didn't. He sat down on the small couch next to it.

"Is it okay if I sit here?" I asked, pointing at it like a five-year-old kid pointing out his favorite toy at the local toy store.

"Go right ahead," Dr. Forrester responded.

Being the gentleman that I sometimes try to be, I waited for the doctor to sit down before doing the same.

I felt a little foolish about being so excited over something as ridiculous as the chair that my rear end was resting upon, but I reminded myself that I've done some of my best crime solving while sitting in my easy chair. It seems to somehow get my analytical juices flowing. Considering the circumstances, I guess it would be appropriate for me to say that it's become a kind of security blanket to me.

Dr. Forrester started us off by letting us know how devastated she felt over the little girls' deaths. She told us that nothing in her career could ever be as important as helping us catch the killer.

Then I gave her the rundown on Lisa Sanchez and the alleged dreams that she'd been having.

"I'm afraid that I can't help you on that one. Dreams of the type that she claimed to be having can have many different interpretations. Keep in mind that there's also the possibility that she could have been fabricating the entire story."

"But why would she do that?" I asked.

"Again, there could be a number of different reasons. She could possibly be trying to protect someone, or perhaps she could be trying to trap you."

"Trap me into what?"

"Into falling for her. Falling for her vulnerability. She could be trying to get you on her side for some reason."

She did trap me. I'd been fantasizing about her ever since that day she came to my office.

Earl brought up my suggestion from the previous day regarding reaching out to the guy via the media.

The doctor sat there silently for a minute or so before responding.

"It's extremely important that we always keep in mind that we're not dealing with a rational person. What we have here is an extremely disturbed individual who undoubtedly gets a great deal of satisfaction from the control that he has, not only over his victims, but over the rest of us as well. I think that trying to open the lines of communication with him could very well pose a threat to that sense of control. He needs to feel as though he's the one who's calling all the shots. It's quite likely that he suffered through a severely abusive childhood, against which he was completely defenseless. So any loss of control that he perceives over this situation could further escalate his feelings of helplessness and make him even more of a danger."

It looked like the Sarge was right once again.

"I do strongly suggest, however, that you try to open up all lines of communication, including via the media, with this young lady that you've spoken about. I would also recommend that Detective Miller be directly involved in this, since he was the one that she sought out. There might be a reason that she did that."

I hadn't given it a minute's thought until the doctor said that. Why did she ask to speak with me, specifically, when there were over forty Nassau and Suffolk detectives on the case?

"I, too, should be directly involved," the doctor went on to say. "If it is fear that's immobilizing her from helping us catch this person, then we have to be very careful not to make her any more frightened than she already is. She needs to have complete and unconditional trust in us."

We spent the remaining time filling Dr. Forrester in on the confessions that Father Vecchia received. The doctor seemed just as puzzled as I had been when I told her that the lady at the second confession couldn't have been Lisa Sanchez. She, like myself, was very doubtful that there was more than one woman giving this same confession.

When I told her that it just so happened that Father Vecchia was someone that I'd known for my entire life, she said that she wasn't so sure that it was necessarily a coincidence.

"You may be the reason that she chose Father Vecchia to confess to. The woman might have been hoping that he'd tell you about it afterwards."

"This," she went on to say, "is only speculation. But we shouldn't rule it out completely, by any means."

There was something in the back of my mind that finally came forward, just as the Sarge and I were about to leave.

"One other thing, Dr. Forrester. The fifth victim, Briane Rodgers, had an identical twin who was with her at the time of her abduction."

"Yes, I do remember seeing that on the news."

"Do you think that she's at risk?"

She thought for a moment and then, in a voice that

matched the saddened look on her face, she said, "Until this person is apprehended, Detective Miller, I'm afraid that every little girl is at risk."

CHAPTER 30

During our drive back to the precinct, my mind began to wander once again. I started thinking about what it would be like if my estranged daughter Jill and I were sitting in Dr. Forrester's office, trying to make amends. I hadn't seen or spoken with Jill in nearly eighteen years, so I was having a hard time of it because I wasn't able to picture what she looked like as an adult.

So instead of focusing on the here and now, my thoughts drifted into the past. Once upon a time, I was the coach of Jill's PAL soccer team. She couldn't have been more than nine or ten at the time. In the final game of the season, which was to decide the league's champion, Jill scored the winning goal in overtime. As soon as the ball landed in the goal, she started looking around for me. Well, there I was, with my arms wide open. With that shy little grin sprawled across her adorable face, she raced across the field to embrace me.

We hugged each other. Then I lifted her up and onto my shoulders.

Her teammates gathered around us, chanting "Jill! Jill! Jill!" They must have gone on for ten minutes, nonstop.

It was a Kodak moment, if ever there was one.

I don't think I've experienced a moment like that since then. One that's so unforgettable that the vividness with which I remember every detail makes it seem as though it happened only yesterday.

That one evening, many years ago, when my mother sat us down in the living room to tell us about the phone call that she just received will always be my most unforgettable one, though.

As a New York City homicide detective, my father knew that every day on the job could be his last. He used to tell us as much, pretty often. I think that he wanted to forewarn us, to help lessen the pain, should it actually happen. I don't believe that anything could have made it less painful, though. Life itself can be painful enough for a sixteen-year-old kid. Having your father shot dead in the line of duty can make it damn near unbearable.

I got myself so upset thinking about my estranged daughter

and deceased father that I stopped at the Gateway Pub on my way home from the precinct, because I didn't feel like sitting at home alone with my thoughts. I didn't get there until about seven-thirty, and I had to wait a little while until an empty barstool became available. Rather than my usual draft, I ordered a double vodka, straight up. I downed it pretty fast. Then I ordered a couple more.

After I gulped down the last one, the anesthetic effect kicked in. Jill and dad drifted back into my subconscious.

Then, for some godforsaken reason, I stood up, walked out the front door and drove to a place called Time to Unwind. This happens to be the place where my darling Kerri was gainfully employed.

Most people just take for granted that Time to Unwind is where Kerri and I first met. They happen to be mistaken. We met at Bethpage State Park, at the golf course there, the same place that hosts the U.S. Open.

It was during a charity tournament for Schneider Children's Hospital, which is a hospital where little kids with real big health problems, cancer being the dominant one, go for treatment and if they're fortunate enough, where they recuperate afterwards.

When I got home from the tournament, I realized that I had driven home without my golf clubs. I'd left them in the pick-up area, next to the parking lot. When I went back to get them, they weren't there. Kerri, who had volunteered to help out at the tournament, had taken them into the clubhouse, where they'd be safe.

For a golf lover like me, saving one's golf clubs is almost equivalent to saving the life of a loved one. When I asked her, half in jest, what I could possibly do to repay her, she said, "Well, you can give me a ride in that Corvette of yours. I've never driven in one before."

So, with the top down and the sun beating down upon us, we drove around the Island for hours. We circled around Jones Beach and Robert Moses Beach, and then headed out east, all the way to Mattituck on the North Fork. We stopped to do a little wine tasting at one of the vineyards out there before heading back to Bethpage.

It wasn't until our third date that I found out what she did for

70

a living. By that time, I'd already grown pretty fond of her. If I would have found out sooner, I'm not so sure that I would have pursued the relationship.

CHAPTER 31

After paying the twenty-dollar cover charge at the door, I stepped inside and gave the place a quick looking-over. It was a lot classier looking than I had imagined. There were mirrors all over the place and purple crushed-velvet carpet covering the floors. I sat down at one of the many small tables surrounding the large center stage where the girls were dancing. There were four young ladies up there. Kerri wasn't one of them.

I glanced around the place, looking for her. She was nowhere in sight. I looked down at my watch. It was around nine o'clock, which seemed like a reasonable time for her to be on a dinner break, being that she started her shift at five.

Man, was I mistaken!

There she was, walking out of some back room holding some guy's hand.

I stood up and walked right over to them. I'll never forget the look on Kerri's face when she saw me. She let go of the guy's hand, fast.

"Who the fuck is this guy?" I screamed.

The guy took off for the front door like a bat out of hell.

"What are you doing here, Max?"

"That doesn't answer my question, damn it."

She grabbed hold of my hand and led me over to one of the tables. Then she pulled two chairs together and said, "Sit down, Max, please."

I obeyed.

"Max, I was giving the guy a private lap dance. I made fifty bucks in ten minutes."

"You never told me you're a lap dancer."

"I'm an exotic dancer, Max. Exotic dancers are also lap dancers in this day and age. I figured that a cop, of all people, would have known this."

"Well, you figured wrong because this particular cop thought that a stripper was a stripper and a lap dancer was a lap dancer. So, what the hell were you doing holding his hand?"

"Would you rather that I be fucking him? The guy just paid me fifty bucks for nothing, so I let him hold my hand for a minute or two. Big deal!"

"He didn't pay you for doing nothing."

"All right, he paid me for grinding my knee into his balls and wiggling my tits in front of his face. Does that make you feel better?"

I broke down and started laughing so hard that I nearly fell off my chair.

"What the hell's so funny?"

"You ground your knee into his balls?"

"That's what we were taught to do, grind and wiggle. Wanna try one?"

"No thanks. What I really want to do is to go home and get some sleep."

"You've been drinking, haven't you?"

"A little."

"Drive home slow and safely, Max. Okay?"

"Fast and crazy, got ya, sweetheart."

"I mean it, Max!"

When I stood up, Kerri grabbed hold of my hand and walked me to the front door.

"Better get some sleep now, mister, while you've still got a chance."

"I will, but you've got to promise me something first."

"Name it."

"Promise me that you'll get all those knee grinds out of your system before you come home."

CHAPTER 32

The liquor in me turned the whole situation surrounding Kerri and her lap dancing into one big joke. But I sure wasn't laughing when I woke up the next morning. So I decided to give it a couple of days, to see if my feelings would change.

They didn't. So the following night, I set my alarm clock for two-thirty to make sure that I was awake when she got home.

"What are you doing up?" she asked as she placed her pocketbook on the glass table in the foyer.

I sat up in my easy chair and clicked off the television.

"Have a seat, Kerri. Please."

At a snail's pace, she made her way to the couch and sat down, eyeballing me every step of the way.

"Is something wrong, Max?"

I was just about to speak when, all of a sudden, tears came gushing out of me.

Kerri walked over and wrapped her arms around me.

"What's wrong, Max? What's wrong?"

Then, of all things, she took off her top and started wiping up my tears with it. I felt like an infant being consoled by his mommy before breastfeeding time. It was undoubtedly a most pathetic sight. So I shot up and hurried over to the bathroom and threw some cold water on my face, to awaken the man in me.

Then I walked back into the living room and sat down on the couch, next to Kerri and her boobs. I looked her straight in the eye and said, "I have a daughter."

"Really?"

"Yeah, really."

"How come you never told me?"

"Probably for the same reason that you never told me that you're a lap dancer."

For the first time since I met her, Kerri was speechless.

"I haven't seen her in a long, long time."

Kerri sat there in silence. Then, she asked, "How old is she?"

"Older than you."

"That's pretty old."

"I've decided that I'm going to try and locate her soon. I've been missing her terribly lately."

After another brief silence, Kerri asked, "How come all of a sudden, after so many years?"

It took me a moment to think of the proper answer.

"Because I'm her father, that's why."

Then, just like I had rehearsed, I did a backward countdown in my mind, before I said it. Three, two, one, go!

"I'd like you to move out, Kerri."

She didn't respond at first. Then she asked the obvious.

"May I ask why?"

"Well, as you know, this case is taking a heavy toll on me, in more ways than one."

"I know it is Max, but...."

"It's forced me to take some good, hard looks in the mirror and do you know what I've been seeing?"

With tears trickling down her face, Kerri shook her head.

"I've seen a fifty-three year old man who abandoned his daughter years ago. I've also seen a pathetic excuse of a man who's living with a fucking lap dancer half his age."

"Is that what this is all about? You resent the fact that I'm a lap dancer?"

"Let's just say that it doesn't exactly help matters."

"Well, I'm sure as hell not about to stop, if that's what you'd like."

"What I'd really like is to know when you're going to be out of here."

With her big boobs wiggling all over the place, Kerri stormed into the bedroom. She emerged a little while later, dragging a suitcase. She stopped by the glass table and picked up her pocketbook. Then she opened it up and took the house key off of her key chain.

Without saying a word, she turned and threw it at me with all her might.

I ducked to avoid being hit.

When I looked back up, she was gone.

CHAPTER 33

A few days later, Claude insisted that I have dinner at his home. He told me that he didn't like the idea of me dining alone.

"I've been eating alone almost every night as it is. Kerri had to leave for work before I got home at night. You know that, Claude."

"Hey, Max, Florence and the kids would love to have you over. So how about if you do it for them. Okay?"

Claude sure knew my weak spot.

"Okay, for them, I'll do it."

Through the tone of my voice, I wanted my partner to understand that in no uncertain terms did my acceptance of his invitation have anything to do with him. Why? Because I knew that the truth of the matter was that Claude's dinner invitation had very little to do with how I was feeling about Kerri's departure, and a whole lot to do with how he was feeling about it.

For Claude, Kerri's moving out was cause for celebration.

This is not to say that Claude disliked Kerri personally. To this day, I don't believe that to be the case. It was what Kerri symbolized to him that caused his ill feelings towards her. She symbolized the streets that Claude grew up on.

Claude was a very proud man. He was proud of where he came from, and he was proud of who he became. Although growing up on the streets of the East New York section of Brooklyn does not, in itself, deserve bragging rights, it did for my partner.

Claude, being the type of person that he is, was able to rid himself of those streets. Your average Joe, like me, who grew up in some lily-white Long Island town, usually has no way of truly appreciating what a tremendous accomplishment that is. I was lucky, though. My father brought those streets into our home. That's where he spent his working day. He gave us a flavor of what they were like. What amazed my dad more than anything else, he used to tell us, were the kids who resisted the temptations of the quick, easy bucks to be made on those streets - the Claude Greers.

Unlike most other city kids, who became *city* cops after being lucky enough to beat the streets, Claude decided to become a cop in nearby Nassau County. His reasons were understandable, his main one being that he had already spent enough time fearing for his life on a daily basis. His other reason, to use Claude's exact terminology: "It's a place where the paychecks and the houses are a whole lot bigger."

I've been keeping a little secret from Claude ever since we became partners eleven years ago. Claude became my partner because I had requested it. I also happened to be the one who recommended that he be made detective. I made the request because of his excellent police performance and because I knew that he came from the same place that my father once worked, the streets.

If Claude would have known this, there's no way that he would have gone along with it. Claude was dead set against being given any special treatment because of who he was or where he came from.

Hey dad, you were right once again. Claude Greer is one very special person.

CHAPTER 34

My evening at the Greers' turned out to be a most enjoyable one. Florence's cooking was second to none, just like always. After dinner, we all sat around the living room. Pam and Tamara did a little duet for me of a few songs that they sing in their church choir. It was real sweet of them, and I certainly enjoyed hearing the sound of their pretty little voices. But like a lot of things those days, it brought back memories of Jill. She absolutely loved to sing when she was their age.

When I returned home from the Greers' warmth and hospitality, Sparky was every bit as excited to see me as I was to have him there, waiting to greet me. With Kerri now gone, it was just the two of us once again.

After tending to Sparky's needs, I sat down in my easy chair and flicked on the boob tube. There was nothing on. It wouldn't have mattered much if there was. My attention span was on par with that of a two-year-old; images of Kerri were beginning to surface in my mind. I started picturing her as she looked the day that I met her for the first time, with that long brown hair, those long, shapely legs and that bright, wide smile that could make even the most bitter of souls feel a little kinder.

It didn't take me long to realize that, just like the other night, I was in no mood to be sitting at home, accompanied by nothing but thoughts of the past. This time, though, I wasn't about to pay a surprise visit to Kerri. Once was more than enough.

So what I did was, I went outside, popped down the roof of my Corvette, and went for a cruise. I wound up taking the same drive that I had taken with Kerri on the day that I first met her.

On the way back this time, however, I took a detour to the Rodgers' residence at 42 Denmar Street in Farmingdale. I sat in front of their house, staring at it for quite a while. The dreamer in me was hoping to get some kind of miraculous flash of insight into the case by being there, also known in musical jargon as "dreaming the impossible dream."

Eventually, a plain clothes cop in an undercover cop car pulled along side of me.

"Can I help you with something, pal?" he asked.

I took out my badge and held it up for him to see.

"Anything out of the ordinary to report, Officer?" I asked him.

"An occasional sightseer here and there, but other than that, nothing at all, Detective."

After shooting the bull for a little while, I glanced at my watch and saw that it was approaching eleven p.m., so I bid the officer farewell and headed home.

I kept tossing and turning in my bed that night, unable to fall asleep. So I downed a couple of sleeping pills. Not exactly my ordinary bedtime diet, but I knew darn well, that the next day was not exactly going to be a very ordinary one.

I figured that I'd need a good night's sleep, at the very least, to help get me through it.

CHAPTER 35

The long-awaited buzz of my intercom came at a little past one, the following afternoon.

"We're ready for ya, Max."

So I grabbed my cup of coffee and walked down the hallway to the Sarge's office.

Dr. Forrester was seated on one of the steel-framed chairs across from him. She stood up and greeted me with a warm smile when I entered the room and extended her hand to me as I approached. I shook it, real gently. As I did so, a bright wide smile surfaced on my face.

I eyeballed the formal looking black pantsuit that she was wearing. It made her look like some kind of corporate C.E.O., which is not to say that she was no longer a pleasant sight to behold.

As soon as I sat down on the steel-framed chair next to hers, she got down to business.

"With a little bit of luck, today could very well precipitate the turning point of this investigation. For that to happen, it's essential that we get our message across to Ms. Sanchez, and anyone else who might be of help to us, as effectively as possible."

The doctor turned her eyes away from the Sarge and towards me as she spoke. She did so for good reason - the "we" she was referring to was none other than yours truly.

Then she leaned over and took a few sheets of typewritten paper out of her attaché case. She handed one apiece to the Sarge and me and kept one for herself.

"Before you read the speech that I've written, please keep in mind that Detective Miller will not be reciting it verbatim. Rather, he and I will be making certain revisions to it so that it comes across as though he's the one that's doing the talking."

I was just about to make some childish remark about having to change all the words that contain more than one syllable for that to be the case, but decided that it wasn't the right time for any stupid wisecracks. So I read over the speech. It was real good, perhaps a little too good, which is precisely why Dr.

Forrester said that bit about the two of us making changes to it.

Then, wouldn't you know it, rather than thinking of ways to revise the speech, I started thinking about this moronic coffee commercial that used to be on TV quite often when I was a kid. It would start off with a whole bunch of people in some coffee-producing village, standing around waiting for some guy who, upon his arrival, would walk over to a table, sit down and take a few sips from a coffee cup that was sitting there waiting for him. After doing so, he'd put the cup down and smile. Then he'd nod his head up and down to show his approval.

The people in the village would then dance around in celebration, like a bunch of lunatics.

"The demanding one. When Juan Valdez talks, people listen," a voice would say as the commercial ended.

Although I've only known her for an hour or two at best, Dr. Forrester's speech that I had just read, coupled with the enlightening meeting at her office a few days prior, left no doubt in my mind that I was sitting next to a modern-day Juan Valdez. One who knew a heck of a lot more about the human mind than that guy on TV with the pencil-thin mustache knew about coffee.

Anyway, getting back to the matter at hand, we spent some time revising the speech. Then, when my moment finally arrived, the doctor and I headed down the long hallway towards the precinct's front entrance.

"Ready, Detective?" she asked as we stepped outside.

"Ready or not," I replied.

CHAPTER 36

When I sweat, I do so like a pig in labor, so fortunately, it was a fairly mild August evening. Otherwise I probably wouldn't have stood a chance of getting through it without passing out.

It seemed as though every news team on the planet was there, shining their bright lights in my face.

The butterflies were there as well, eating away at the inside of my stomach. Dr. Forrester had warned me about the butterflies so, unlike the oppressive heat being emitted from those lights, the butterflies were expected.

When the guy finally started the countdown until airtime, I took out my handkerchief and wiped the sweat from my forehead. Then I stepped up to the microphones.

"Ready, go!" he said, pointing his index finger at me.

"Good evening, I'm Detective Max Miller of the Nassau County Police Department. As I'm sure you're all aware, five horrific killings have taken place over the past two months. Four of them occurred here on Long Island, and one occurred some sixty miles north of here, in Rockland County."

I used the brief pause that Dr. Forrester had instructed me to take to wipe some more sweat from my forehead.

"We don't know, nor can we possibly comprehend, why someone would choose to murder these little girls. What we do know is that nothing can ever be as precious to us as our young children. I urge anyone who has any information regarding these murders to call us at the telephone number being displayed on the bottom of your television screen. The number is 1-800-L.I. POLICE. Anyone who even thinks that they might know something about the murders is urged to call us. No child is safe until the killer is caught. I say this for no other reason than because it's the sad truth. On behalf of those little girls whose lives will be saved by your phone calls, I thank you from the bottom of my heart."

Despite the fact that the news people had been informed beforehand that I wouldn't be answering any questions, they began bombarding me with them as soon as I finished speaking.

Rather than acknowledging any of them, I leaned over the microphone and, like Elvis himself, let out a quick and to-the-point "Thank you very much."

Then I turned and walked up the stairs.

CHAPTER 37

An hour or so after my television appearance, I received a phone call from Sister Rosemary.

She called to tell me that Father Stanton had arrived home two days prior. She went on to say that she'd just seen me on the news, and that she probably wouldn't have called so soon if it weren't for that. When I asked why that was the case, she said, "Because of what you said about the possibility of a phone call helping to save some little girl's life. You were right. I'm not saying that Father Stanton will be of any help to you. I certainly don't believe that to be the case. It's just that I felt an obligation to tell you what I did because of what you said on the news."

"Did you tell him that we had stopped by the school?"

"Yes. I told him that you were here. I couldn't remember your partner's name, however."

"Well, I very much appreciate the phone call, Sister Rosemary."

"There's one more thing I like to say, Detective Miller."

"What's that?"

"Thank you for what you're doing."

I was tempted to tell her that there was nothing whatsoever to thank me for. But instead, I let out a cordial, "You're very welcome."

Then we exchanged goodbyes.

Two thoughts crossed my mind as I hung up the phone, one being that the more I spoke with Sister Rosemary, the more I liked her. The other was that I was becoming increasingly impressed with Dr. Forrester; her speech already had an impact, barely an hour after I gave it.

Shortly after I hung up with Sister Rosemary, the Sarge stepped into my office.

"Want to join us for a cup of coffee, or a little something to eat at the diner?" he asked.

I was about to ask him who the "us" was comprised of when Dr. Forrester stepped into the room.

"Sorry about that," she said as she placed her cell phone inside her pocketbook. "I'm ready to go."

The decision was now an easy one.

"Sounds good to me," I said as I stood up from my desk and followed them out the door.

CHAPTER 38

I led the way into the diner and headed to the same booth that Claude and I had sat in the week before.

Dr. Forrester and the Sarge sat down first. I sat across from them.

After we placed our order, with the young, shapely waitress, I said, "I received a phone call from Sister Rosemary. Father Stanton arrived home two days ago."

"How long were you going to wait to tell me?" the Sarge asked, in a tone that clearly expressed his annoyance.

"When did she call to tell you this?" Dr. Forrester asked.

"About an hour or so ago."

"I say that we pay him a visit pronto," the Sarge said.

"I'm not sure if that would be the best course of action, at this time," the doctor replied.

"Then what do you suggest?" the Sarge asked.

"I suggest that someone watch him very closely to try and learn a little more about him, like Detective Greer did with Lisa Sanchez."

"Why not question him right away?" I asked.

"Because, from what you gentlemen have told me, it appears to be doubtful that he's actually the killer. So questioning him right away might actually do more harm than good."

"How so?" the Sarge asked, beating me to the punch.

"Because I think that if he knows anything about the murders, and I have no idea if that is, indeed, the case, he'll be inclined to remain tight-lipped about it. Questioning him right now might cause his defenses to build up, thus making him clam up even more. One's actions, however, often do their talking for them. So I say that you hold off talking to him until after you've observed him for awhile. I also think that if he does indeed know something, then the question of why he's held off telling us is a lot more likely to be answered by his actions than his words."

The doctor took a few sips of her coffee and slowly placed down the cup, just like Juan Valdez did on that commercial. And just like the people of that little coffee-producing village, I wanted to jump for joy over having "the demanding one" on our side.

CHAPTER 39

I must have been dreaming about something real pleasurable because I was more ticked off than ever at being woken, in the middle of the night, by the ringing of my telephone.

"Hello," I said, quite inhospitably.

"Detective Max Miller?" the muffled voice on the other end of the line asked.

"Yeah, who is this?" I snapped back, like a guy who'd just been woken up at the ungodly hour that it was.

"Well, I bet that I know who you were wishing it to be, Detective."

Bingo!

"I'm sorry, but I'm having a very hard time hearing you," I said, trying my hardest to come off real nice and polite.

"You know, Detective, you really should do something about that perspiration problem of yours. It's really quite unsightly. Almost made me want to change the channel."

An irritating little chuckle followed.

"May I ask with whom I'm speaking?"

"You sound so very prim and proper for an oversized, brainless wonder like yourself, Detective. I've gotta get going now, but before I do, may I ask you one quick question, Detective?"

"Sure, go ahead," I replied as politely as was possible, after having listened to that unflattering description of myself.

"Where'd you find that fat-assed partner of yours, the Bronx Zoo?"

A burst of laughter preceded the loud buzz of the dial tone.

Although I was all but positive that the length of the call wasn't long enough to be traced, I wasn't about to take any chances, so I immediately called the precinct to be sure.

When Lauren, the nighttime operator responded with a slow and monotone, "Wasn't even close, I'm sorry Max," it put that matter to rest in a hurry.

So I leaned over and hung up the phone. Then I slid back in my bed until my back was against the headboard. I remained in that position, playing back the conversation over and over again in my mind.

It seemed pretty much a given at that point that whoever it was who made that phone call knew who I was before I appeared on the evening news. That remark about Claude told me that much. But the remark about knowing whom I wished it to be was a different story entirely. I obsessed over it until I eventually fell asleep with my back still flush against the wall.

A few hours later, I woke up in that same position, with that remark still sitting on the top of my mind. Who did I wish it to be? Lisa Sanchez, perhaps? If it was Ms. Sanchez whom he was referring to, then the chances of the caller being the real McCoy were, needless to say, pretty darn good. I knew, however, that the chances were also pretty darn good that the caller could have been one of the many undesirables that Claude and I had locked up over the years, finally getting a little payback at us.

It wasn't until around the time that I pulled into the precinct's parking lot, almost two hours later, that my mind took a break from fixating on the phone call that I received. I kept on thinking, however, that Lisa Sanchez certainly wasn't the only one that I'd have wished it to be. I was missing Jill more than ever.

CHAPTER 40

He sat in his black Honda, in the far corner of the parking lot.

He couldn't take his eyes off them, Briana and her campmates, running around the small fenced-in playground, going from slide to swings to seesaw and back again. Round and round they went. The strong summer heat was not slowing them down one bit.

"The Hangman's been to London. The Hangman's been to France. The Hangman will hang Briana without her underpants."

The others couldn't control themselves. Their laughter grew louder as his words echoed in his mind.

The counselors were keeping a very watchful eye on the girls, making the playground out of bounds for now. The string lay nestled around his left hand nonetheless.

He remained there for quite some time, not taking his eyes off of them for a second. Eventually, they lined up in pairs and marched out of the playground, and then out of view.

As he slowly drove out of the parking lot, he reached forward and turned on his CD player. His song began to play. So he pressed down on the accelerator and headed for the parkway.

When his favorite part of the song came on, he turned the volume way up. "Show me the way to the next little girl, oh don't ask why, oh don't ask why. For when we find the way to the next little girl, I tell you, she will die. I tell you, she will die."

His voice drowned out Jim Morrison's as he sang aloud, occasionally changing the lyrics to better suit his taste.

He continued west on the parkway, that same song playing over and over again.

"Show me the way to the next little girl, with straight hair or with curls, she's the Hangman's little girl."

The others giggled themselves into near hysterics.

Their laughter subsided by the time that he exited the parkway and headed north, to the Land of AB&C Day Camp in the town of Baldwin.

CHAPTER 41

Claude was sitting across from me, with his arms folded and his feet upon my desk, as I gave him the blow-by-blow details of the middle-of-the-night phone call that I received. He was quite amused by what the caller had to say about me. I figured he'd have the same reaction when I started telling him about what the guy said about him.

Man, was I mistaken!

No sooner did I get the words out that he jumped up and headed for the door.

"Let's go Max, move your ass!" he screamed.

By the time we got outside, Claude was moving at a pace that would be justly classified as something between a jog and a full sprint. For Claude, however, it was the fastest that those tree-trunk-like legs of his would allow.

When we got to Old Country Road, Claude turned on the siren. He was driving faster than usual, and Claude has never exactly been a slouch behind the wheel.

"You want to at least give me a hint as to what's going on here?" I yelled, loud enough to be heard above the screeching grind of the siren.

"We're going to make sure that my kids are safe."

"Why wouldn't they be?"

Claude glanced over at me.

"Jesus Christ, Max. Someone calls in the middle of the fucking night, right after you appear on the news, and starts making comments about me. That makes me real nervous. Do you know why, Max?"

He continued without pausing, making it rather obvious that he had no interest in hearing my response.

"Because I have something that he's after: young daughters."

"Yeah, but what makes you think that he'll go after your kids?"

"Because, plain and simple, the guy's a fucking lunatic. You can't try rationalizing the behavior of a psychopathic lunatic like this guy."

"I don't know, Claude. Do you really think that he's our guy? I mean, why the hell would he call me at home? Not exactly the best of moves, you know."

"Think about this one, Max. Since when does a fucking lunatic child killer concern himself with doing what's best?"

CHAPTER 42

His smirk gave way to a smile at the very sight of it, the police car sitting there, just beyond the confines of the campgrounds. Its flashing overhead light barely visible against the powerful bright rays of the strong summer sun.

"Just as I suspected, they think that everyone's as stupid as they are. For heaven's sake, Dumb and Dumber had better step aside and let those two imbeciles get in front of them."

The boisterous laughter of the others echoed in his head until he could take it no longer.

"Shut up, you babbling fools!"

Then he picked up his cell phone and dialed. He waited patiently for the sound of the beep.

"Detective Miller, I must say, I've seen ignoramuses in my time, but you guys take the cake. Do you really think that I'm stupid enough to go after those little jungle bunnies while you two baboons are sitting there watching them? Use your brain, Detective. If you have one, that is."

The others had never done it before - applauded him. But they knew that the time for ovations was now upon them.

"Bravo! Encore! Encore! More, more, we want more!"

He felt quite moved by their display of affection. So much so, in fact, that he picked the phone back up and hit the redial button.

"Hello there, Detective, it's your number one fan once again. Please excuse me for having forgotten to ask the first time, but hey, big guy, how's she hanging?"

As he placed down his phone, he bowed his head to acknowledge another round of their thunderous applause.

CHAPTER 43

There was a sheet of the Sarge's memo paper taped to the door of my office when my partner and I arrived back at the precinct. Claude, who was walking a step ahead of me, read what it had to say first. After I took my turn, Claude lifted up his arm to show me the time on his watch: 3:59 p.m. is what it said.

We looked at each other and grinned. Written on the sheet of memo paper was, "Meeting in my office at 4pm, sharp."

So off to the Sarge's office we went.

Dr. Forrester was there, seated across from him. I, being a good deal older than my partner, sat down next to her on the one remaining chair. Claude stood behind us with his arms folded.

"Claude, why don't you grab a chair from next door?" the Sarge suggested.

"Nah, I'm fine, Sarge."

Then, all of a sudden, Claude stepped forward and said, "For the sake of my family, I'd like your permission to be taken off the case, Sarge."

A thousand different feelings hit me all at once. But what I felt more than anything was an overwhelming sense of relief for Claude. He must have been worried even worse than he had let on, and *that* was pretty darn bad.

"I will say that you caught me a little off guard, Claude. But I do understand your concern for your family's welfare. So yes, you're off the case," the Sarge replied.

Claude whispered a barely audible, "Thanks, Sarge."

Then, he bid the doctor a polite farewell and walked towards the door.

"Catch ya in a little while, Max," he said as he headed out the door.

Simultaneously, the Sarge and Dr. Forrester turned their heads to look at me. Through their eyes I could read their thoughts.

"I had no idea that was coming," I replied to their unspoken inquiry.

"Really?" Dr. Forrester said.

"Really! No idea whatsoever."

"You must be a bit surprised that he didn't discuss it with you beforehand."

"He didn't know, beforehand. Believe me."

"I do," the doc replied.

I glanced up at the Sarge. He was staring straight into space, looking as if he was a million miles away.

When he snapped out of it, he looked at us and said, "I think we'll save our meeting for another time."

CHAPTER 44

Sparky wasn't the only one to welcome me home that evening. The two messages left on my answering machine by my psychotic phone buddy were there to greet me as well.

I darned near fainted, when I listened to them. Claude's fatherly instinct was, eerily, right on target. The guy was at his daughters' camp at the very same time that we were there. He must have been watching us the whole time.

Although the guy's voice was still quite muffled, there was something about it that began to give me the feeling that I may have heard it before, other than during his middle of the night call, that is.

But no matter how many times I played it over, I still wasn't certain as to whether or not its familiarity was anything more than a figment of my overanxious imagination.

When Sparky finally lost his patience and started scratching his paw on my dresser, I hurried to get his leash and take him outside. Sparky's paw on the furniture was his way of saying, "Last chance before I take care of business on your carpet."

As I strolled down the block with my beloved canine a step ahead of me, I knew that this was another one of those evenings that wasn't meant to be spent indoors, watching television. At the beach, watching the sunset was much more like it. So I opened the passenger door of my Vette to let Sparky in. His thick, brown tail started wagging back and forth as he jumped inside and turned, round and round, until he found a comfortable position to sit himself down in.

Then I opened my garage door and removed the plastic wrapping from the unopened beach chair that I had purchased a few months prior. I usually head to the beach quite often at this time of the year, but this summer was a different story entirely.

Although Jones Beach is closer to my home, I decided to head east and drive the five or so extra miles to Robert Moses Beach because dogs are unofficially permitted there during the evening hours.

As I lay there, semi-reclined in my bright blue beach chair, with my sandals off and Sparky lying in the sand beside me, I stared straight into the Atlantic. Like I often do when I'm alone at the beach, I started thinking about what this short, strange journey known as life is all about. I'm not totally convinced about that "Big Guy in the Sky" story; it never struck me as being real believable. To me, it seems like an interesting bit of fiction, which many people treat as fact, because it gives them a sense of security. But then again, maybe I'm the one who's out of touch with the true story. Who knows?

Usually, the beach is the one place where I'm able to totally clear my mind of my police work for a few hours, other than on the golf course, I should say. But peace of mind doesn't come easily while little girls are being hanged to death. So my brief "what's it all about" moment of contemplation was the only moment during my hour and a half stay at the beach that wasn't spent thinking about the case.

Claude's sudden announcement earlier in the day had thrown me for quite a loop. Those two phone messages that the guy left while he was somewhere on the outskirts of Claude's daughters' camp threw me for an even bigger one.

I knew that the Sarge would probably throw a fit if he found out that I was lying on the beach, rather than rushing to submit the cassette tape from my answering machine. But I wanted some more time to listen to that voice. Maybe something would hit me if I listened to it enough times.

Then I started thinking about something Dr. Forrester had said, about there being a very real possibility that Lisa Sanchez intentionally came to me, as opposed to any of the other detectives on the case. Why would she do so? I just couldn't figure that one out for the life of me.

When the sun eventually made its way beyond the horizon, I woke Sparky up and headed back home.

Later that night, I listened to the tape over and over again. What resulted was a pounding migraine, and nothing more.

CHAPTER 45

After submitting the tape from my answering machine to the tech department, I headed to the conference room for our scheduled 10:00 a.m. meeting. The conference room is actually nothing more than an ordinary-looking office that shares a one-way, mirrored window with the office next to it. Its primary purpose is to hold interrogations.

There were four attendees at the meeting other than myself: the lovely Dr. Forrester, the Sarge and Detectives Guy Saladino and Wayne McCorry, who were the ones that the Sarge had chosen to keep a watch on Father Stanton.

Wayne McCorry is real tall, about six-ten, and very thin as well. He also possesses a complexion that has got to be among the fairest that I've ever laid my eyes upon. One look at the guy and there's no need to ask how he's come to be known, by most, as "Noodle." His partner, Guy Saladino is a medium-built Italian-American who looks exactly like the stereotypical one: dark eyes, slicked-back hair, olive complexion and all. One night a number of years ago, Detective Saladino and I almost came to blows when I answered a nuisance call at O'Reilly's Pub in Valley Stream. As it turned out, the nuisance was an overly intoxicated off-duty Officer Saladino. The level of hostility that we harbor towards one another over that little incident has diminished over the years, which is not to say that he's now one of my favorite people on the planet.

It felt weird not having my partner at the meeting, kind of like I was missing my left arm. We had already stationed an officer in front of his house 24-7, as well as one at the day camp, to be sure that his kids were safe.

After we were all seated at the long, rectangular table, Detective Saladino started us off by saying, "Detective McCorry and I don't have a whole heck of a lot to report at this point, because the guy pretty much stayed inside the school building all three days."

Then, Noodle said, "He left the building yesterday at about four in the afternoon for a couple of hours. That was it."

I started to speak, just as Noodle was about to continue. So he glanced at me and I gave him a little nod to let him know that he still had the floor.

"He went to a coffee shop a block or so from the school."

"Did he walk or drive there?" the Sarge asked.

"Walked," said Noodle.

"We're pretty certain that..."

All of a sudden, Claude came barging into the room. He had a much more somber look on his face then he did when he stormed into my office to tell me about the witness at Bear Mountain.

"That damn motherfucker struck again. This time he grabbed her right out of her own backyard."

Then he looked over at the Sarge and said, "Off the case? My big, fat, black ass! Max and I are gonna get this motherfucker. We'll catch this goddamn creep. Believe me, we will!"

CHAPTER 46

The following morning, Claude and I drove to the home of the latest victim, Tara Shiver. She lived in Old Brookville, an upscale little village not too far from Muttontown, which is where his first victim, Alisha Marizzo, had lived.

After Claude parked the car in the long circular driveway, we headed straight to the backyard. We flashed our badges in plain view of the two officers that were stationed there.

"Police Line, Do Not Cross" signs were posted all over the place. We walked over and took a look around the playground, which stood in the rear of the yard. Then we ventured into the woods beyond. We couldn't see any visible signs of tire tracks, which confirmed the findings in the report that was issued by the detectives, who were the first to arrive at the scene. No tire tracks meant that he more than likely parked on the deserted street, just beyond the woods. As I looked down that long, tree-lined street, I couldn't help but think that this guy sure wasn't stupid, not by a long shot. He seemed to know exactly how not to get caught. He had abducted Tara from her own backyard and driven some twenty-five miles east, where he found a suitable place to lynch her. He managed to do so without leaving a stitch of obvious evidence behind.

Since there seemed to be nothing further to be gained by venturing around the outer premises any longer, we headed to the front door of the house. When we arrived there, we stomped our shoes on the doormat to get rid of the dirt that they'd accumulated during our stroll through the woods.

Shortly after Claude rang the doorbell, a young Hispanic woman opened the door. She politely introduced herself as the Shivers' housekeeper, Lucille.

The floor of the spacious foyer area that she led us through was covered by a tiger skin rug, the size of which I'd never before seen.

We followed her down a long hallway. When we came upon the entrance of the living room at the end of the hallway, she stopped and turned to face us.

"Please wait here for a moment," she whispered, before disappearing into the room.

A brief moment later, she reappeared and said softly, "Please come with me."

The victim's parents and brother were sitting on a finely crafted Victorian sofa in the far left corner of the room, just beyond the fireplace. Seated across from them were Tara's grandparents. We slowly walked over to them. The closer that we got, the more distant Mrs. Shiver appeared.

The little boy looked to be the spitting image of his father: same light brown hair, same strong chin. Mr. Shiver stood up as we approached. As we exchanged introductions with him, Claude and I expressed our sympathy. Then I turned and faced the grandparents, and politely asked them if we could be alone with Tara's parents and brother for a little while.

After they exited the room, Mr. Shiver turned to his son and said, "Derek, stand up for a minute, buddy."

He introduced us to the young chap and then asked us to have a seat on the couch across from them.

"Derek has something that he'd like to tell you," he said.

The kid looked up at his old man, who gave his nod of approval.

"I think I saw the guy," little Derek said in a soft, almost apologetic tone of voice.

Claude and I looked at each other and grinned. If there was one thing that would have been deemed permissible to be grinning about under those circumstances, it was those beautiful little words that flowed from the lips of that frightened little kid.

My partner and I simultaneously leaned forward on the sofa to get a little closer to the soft-spoken kid.

"How old are you, Derek?" I asked.

"Six."

"Are you a Yankee fan or a Met fan?"

He needed not a second to think about it.

"Yankee."

"Me too," I said, as I stood up to give him a little high five.

"Claude, here, is a Met fan."

"The Yankees are much better than the Mets," the kid replied. He looked over at his old man, who failed miserably at his attempt to return his son's smile. A pleasant little conversation about those one and only New York Yankees then ensued. Little Derek was getting into it, totally. His dad, you could tell, was just going through the motions for little Derek's sake.

"I was named after Derek Jeter!" the boy said.

His enthusiasm told me that he was nice and loosened up, which meant that it was time to get down to business.

"Where were you when you saw the guy, Derek?" I asked.

Derek fell silent for a moment, obviously much preferring to stay on the prior topic.

"In the backyard."

"Where was Tara when you saw him?"

"On the swing."

"Did you see him walk up to Tara?"

"No, I went inside the house because I got scared."

"Derek's mom had stepped inside for a minute, to use the bathroom. That's when it happened," Mr. Shiver said.

This confirmed yet another statement that was in the report.

I debated whether or not to ask the kid why he didn't divulge this information to the detectives that came to his home yesterday, but quickly talked myself out of that one.

"Did you see what he looked like, Derek?"

"He looked like Father Harrington."

Claude and I exchanged quick glances once again.

"That's the priest from our parish," Mr. Shiver added.

"Was it Father Harrington, Derek?"

"No, he was just wearing the same kind of shirt that Father Harrington always wears."

"Did you see his face?"

"No, not really."

"Then how do you know that it wasn't Father Harrington?"

"Because this man wasn't as big and fat as Father Harrington is."

Mr. Shiver nodded his head, to let us know that his kid was on the right track as far as Father Harrington's weight was concerned.

"Did you see what color his hair was, Derek?"

"No."

"Did the guy see you looking at him?"

Derek looked down for a moment and then let out a barely audible, "No."

"Would you mind coming into the backyard with Detective Claude and me, so that you can show us where the man was when you saw him?"

"Okay."

Little Derek led us to the tree that he had seen the guy walk up to. Then he pointed out the swing that Tara was on when it happened.

As we started walking back towards the house, I looked down at little Derek and said, "You know what, Derek? Sometimes, I can get ahold of some real good Yankee tickets."

"Wow! My dad can only get Met tickets, but who the heck wants to see the stupid Mets. They stink."

Once again, Claude and I glanced over at one another. There was no doubt that the smile on my partner's face, as well as the one on mine, were one hundred percent genuine. But just like those little girls that this creep had abducted, those occasional smiles that we managed would vanish in an instant. And just like any of the other little girls on Long Island, who might end up being in the wrong place at the wrong time, those smiles didn't stand a chance of surviving until we caught him.

We said our goodbyes to Derek and his dad, and thanked them for taking the time to meet with us. Doing so left me with a real hollow feeling inside. Given a choice, I would have preferred to have offered my apologies for not having caught the killer.

As we drove back down the narrow, winding roads of Old Brookville, I started thinking about little Derek Shiver and the person that he had seen. Then I got that feeling in my gut. Not the butterflies this time, but rather that same type of gut-feeling that I had last winter, about the guy killing that seventeen-year-old kid. What it was telling me this time was that what scared little Derek Shiver more than anything was the fact that this guy saw Derek staring at him, and Derek knew it.

My gut was in a talkative mood because it also told me that it might not be a bad idea at all for Claude and me to attend little Tara's funeral.

Although I wasn't sure as to whether or not my gut was beginning to get a little carried away with itself, I sure as hell wasn't about to start second-guessing it at that point.

CHAPTER 47

The climate fit the occasion like a custom-made glove: ninety-five degree heat smothered by such an oppressively thick coating of humidity that the act of breathing was no longer something to be taken for granted. On top of the sauna-like atmosphere lay the blistering rays of the strong summer sun that felt like they could easily bake you alive in no time flat.

A mild and pleasant day would not have been much comfort here. At a Little League game or a picnic perhaps, but not at the funeral of a four-year-old child. The tremendous number of people in attendance was no doubt the reason that the ceremony was not being held inside the air-conditioned church that we parked behind, but rather in the large open field beside it.

There were flocks of people gathered around Mr. and Mrs. Shiver and little Derek when we arrived, making it impossible for us to get close enough to pay our respects. My height, however, gave me the advantage of enabling me to see the Shivers sitting there in the front row by looking over the heads of those that were standing in my way.

Mr. Shiver seemed much the same as he did the prior day, still going through the motions, despite the hell that he was living though. Unfortunately, Mrs. Shiver looked much the same as well. The sorrow that had overtaken her was still evident by the blank look on her face and the empty, million-miles-away stare in her eyes. She was lost, no doubt, but hopefully time would allow her to find her way back.

Little Derek was seated next to his dad, with his hands folded. As I stood there, looking over at the young lad, I began to wonder what was going on inside that little head of his. To a six year-old kid, having your sister abducted from your backyard and later hanged to death can be an experience whose degree of fright is much too great to measure. Having possibly made eye contact with the killer just prior to her abduction must have certainly increased the poor little guy's fear level.

Although I still had no way of knowing whether or not that eye-to-eye encounter did, indeed, take place between Derek and the killer, the feeling in my gut was growing stronger and stronger. I was all but positive that little Derek knew more than he was letting on.

Claude and I grabbed seats in the very last row of the thirty-odd rows of cushioned chairs. We sat on opposite sides of the center aisle from one another, in the two chairs that were closest to that aisle.

The first thing to catch my eye after I sat down was the thick, plush turf that surrounded us. When I got Claude's attention, I pointed down to the ground and said, "Looks just like our lawns, huh?"

Claude smiled and pulled a handkerchief out of his back pocket. Then he leaned his head back a bit and placed it over his face. It became soaking wet in a matter of seconds. Seeing that this appeared to give Claude a little escape from the unbearable heat, I did the same. Anything that might bring relief from the sweltering atmosphere, no matter how temporary, was certainly worth a try.

It wasn't until Father Harrington stepped up to the pulpit a little while later that I began to cool off a bit. I now knew what Derek meant about the guy that he saw not being fat enough to be Father Harrington. Not many people on Earth weigh enough to be Father Harrington. He must have been five hundred pounds, easy.

The longer that I looked up at the poor priest, standing there, sweating profusely, the less uncomfortable I felt. Yes, the conditions had become so utterly intolerable that comfort could only be found in seeing someone suffer worse than me.

Despite the fact that the oppressive heat was wreaking havoc on Father Harrington's oversized body, he was still able to deliver the most dazzling sermon that I'd ever heard in my entire life.

"If we stop and think about what it is that upsets us the most about Tara Shiver's passing, is it not our own mortality? Does Tara's short visit to this world not remind us of how brief our own journey here truly is? When we go to bed tonight let us not say a prayer for Tara Shiver, for she is now under the eternal care of the Lord. Let us instead pray that we, too, will someday earn our place in Heaven. Pray not for Tara Shiver, for Tara's

106

prayers have already been answered. Most importantly, pray that this barbaric murderer is caught before he kills again."

I knew that Norman Vincent Peale himself would have been pretty darn impressed with the power of Father Harrington's positive thinking, as well as how eloquently and gracefully he was able to articulate his message.

Unfortunately though, what goes up must come down.

When little Derek stepped up to the pulpit, a silence so deafening tore through the thick, muggy air that people began clearing their throats to make certain that they hadn't lost their sense of hearing.

When Derek spoke of how he would miss his little sister, and of how she didn't have to worry because he would always take good care of their dog, Buster, there was not a dry eye in the place, including Father Harrington's.

But not many in the crowd took little Derek Shiver's speech harder than yours truly. For it was *me,* who should have caught this psychopathic piece of human slime by now. It was *me* who again failed to give protection to those too weak and vulnerable to protect themselves.

And it was *me*, who, at that very moment, wanted more than ever to hold my long-lost daughter in my arms and let her know how very much I missed her.

CHAPTER 48

We'd been following the countless number of cars in the funeral procession down the long country-like roads of Long Island's elite Gold Coast for about twenty minutes. In all that time, it felt as though we had traveled about ninety feet. Considering that the cemetery was over five miles away, I figured that it would be time for my own burial by the time that we arrived there.

A couple of distinctive sounding little beeps that echoed from my cell phone, however, put an end to that kind of thinking in no time flat.

The cell phone that I pulled out of my shirt pocket was programmed to beep as it did when the answering machine in my home was about to receive a message. The tech guys on the force had given the phone to me after those last two messages had been left on my machine. That's when they changed the machine itself. It had taken them forever to transfer my outgoing message onto the other machine, but it was something that had to be done. We didn't want the guy to become overly cautious about what he had to say, if he were to call back and not hear the same message on my machine.

So I held the phone against my ear and pressed in the button that was designed to enable me to hear what was being said.

When I heard his voice come on, I closed my eyes to help me concentrate.

"I must say, Detective, that Father Harrington creature was a rather nauseating sight. Wouldn't you agree? All that was needed was an apple in that fat mouth of his. In case you've never tasted roast pig, I will tell you this, Detective. It's absolutely scrumptious. Now, as far as you're concerned, Detective, that was quite a display of unmanliness that you put on there. Who would have known what a true sissy you really are? Cha cha, Detective."

I clicked off the phone and instructed Claude to drive up to the hearse at the front of the line. As he did so, I told him what I'd just heard.

When we caught up with the hearse, I rolled down my

window and flashed my badge at the driver. Then I signaled for him to pull over.

The other cars slowly began to follow suit.

What our next move was to be was not an easy decision for us. We could ask little Derek to walk with us, car by car, to see if anyone looked to be the guy that he saw in his backyard. One of many problems with that, though, was that Derek hadn't admitted to seeing the guy's face. Although I personally doubted it quite a bit, there was always the possibility that he didn't get a good look at the guy.

The choice of doing nothing at all, so as not to upset the Shiver family any further, had one rather obvious drawback. It left wide open the possibility that we'd be letting the guy get away from us.

The course of action that my partner and I eventually agreed upon was to walk up to each and every car and take a quick look inside, to see if anyone looked like they didn't belong. Such as a badly deranged psychopath who gets his kicks from butchering little girls and then watching them hang to death.

CHAPTER 49

With overhead lights flashing from atop the half-dozen patrol cars that answered our call for backup, my partner and I began our descent upon the long row of cars.

As luck would have it, the two-lane road that we were standing upon had recently been paved. So on top of everything else, we had to be sure not to stand in any one place for too long a period of time. Otherwise, our shoes might very well become molded into the tar.

Rather than one of us checking out the first half of the cars and the other the second half, we decided to do alternating cars instead. Claude would check out one while I checked the one directly behind it, and so on down the line. We figured that the officers in the patrol cars, who were spread out alongside the procession line, could collectively keep an eye on all of the cars, first to last. This way the guy couldn't stray from the line, no matter where Claude and I happened to be.

We made our way down the line at a fairly brisk pace until the time came that Claude stepped up to car number thirty-one. I knew the car's exact number because we'd been counting them along the way, to make certain that it was that very same number of vehicles that would later pass through the front gates of the cemetery. Claude stood there, engaged in conversation with its driver for quite a while longer than any of the others.

Without stepping away from the car, Claude turned in my direction and yelled out, "Detective Miller, can I see you for a moment, please?"

As I approached, Claude turned his back on the driver in order to look at me.

"Ready for this?" he asked.

"At this point, I think that I'm pretty much ready for anything."

"Maybe not," Claude rebutted.

Then he handed me the driver's license that he'd been looking at.

It took a second for it to register, but when it did, it got the adrenaline pumping, but good. With a shake of my head, I signaled for Claude to step aside so that I could get a good look at the guy.

First impressions being what they are, mine was that if the guy that I was looking at was a sadistic child killer, then I must be Jack the Ripper. He was thin and frail, which made him look quite a bit older than his sixty-eight years, which I had computed from the date of birth shown on his driver's license.

"Good afternoon Father Stanton, I'm Detective Max Miller."

He shook my outstretched hand in a rather weak fashion, and then asked, "Have we met before, Detective? Your name sounds very familiar."

"No, we haven't. But Detective Greer and I were at your school the day after Tracy was murdered."

As soon as I said that, Father Stanton started shaking his head back and forth. About the same time that I got to wondering if his head was ever going to stop shaking, he looked up at me and said, "Tracy was so full of life. She had to have been the most energetic kid that I'd ever known. Such a sweet, sweet child."

"Did you know Tara Shiver, Father?"

"I knew her only as another of the Lord's precious children who perished at the hands of this satanic killer."

The sound of opportunity came knocking upon my mind. Dr. Forrester had said not to interrogate him because it could arouse his suspicions. So I figured that I'd take advantage of the current situation by gently placing the ball in his court.

"Father Stanton, when you're feeling up to it, could you give me a buzz so that we can set up a time when the two of us can sit down together?"

I reached over and handed him my card. He glanced at it, placed it in his shirt pocket and said, "I'll be sure to call you, Detective."

Then in a bit of a melodramatic fashion, I started rummaging through my pockets. Coming up empty-handed, I looked at Claude and said, "You got your cell phone on you? I must have left mine back in the car."

Claude searched through his pockets, or pretended to, I should say.

"Nope, I must have left mine back there, as well."

So I turned around, put my hands on top of Father Stanton's car and leaned down to look at him.

111

"Would you mind if I borrowed your cell phone, Father Stanton? It's for police business."

"I know that I'm well in the minority in this day and age, but I don't own one. Until the day comes that you can pick up one of those little phones and get in touch with 'the man upstairs,' I won't be in need of one either."

I let out a little grin to acknowledge his words of wit. Then I offered him my outstretched hand, which he shook, again with barely a grip.

I made another attempt at trying to catch him off guard by saying, "Better close your window and keep your air conditioner on full blast, Father. It's hot enough to roast a pig out here."

With no sign of uneasiness evident on his face, he said, "You can say that again, Detective."

When his window was fully shut, I turned and glanced over at my partner. Then we looked out yonder at the long line of cars still to go. As we marched towards them, I felt something stuck to the bottom of my shoe.

"Stand still for a second, Claude."

I put my hand on his shoulder, to keep my balance, and then lifted up my foot. Little bits of tar were stuck all over.

"You ain't getting those things off. They're glued right in there," Claude said.

I let go of his shoulder. Then I asked him his thoughts on Father Stanton.

"I'll answer that one after we check out his no-cell-phone story."

"Even if that holds true," I said, "I'd still like to know what the heck he's doing here in the first place, considering that he never heard of Tara Shiver until she was dead."

"Well, maybe he's trying to make up for not being at Tracy's funeral. Killing the guilt, so to speak."

CHAPTER 50

That evening, my phone began to ring just as I was stepping out of the most downright refreshing shower that I'd ever taken in my life. So, dripping wet, I hurried to my bedroom to answer it.

It wasn't the guy's muffled voice that I heard when I picked up the phone this time, but rather, a muffled voice of a member of the female persuasion.

"Detective Max Miller?" she asked.

"Yes. This is Detective Miller."

"Do you know what happened to her?"

"To whom? Do I know what happened to whom?"

Although I tried like hell to sound calm I doubt very much that I succeeded.

"To Lisa Sanchez. Do you know what happened to Lisa Sanchez?"

"No, I don't. Do you?"

After too long a silence, I realized that she was no longer there.

Without putting down the receiver, I clicked off the phone and pressed my finger down on the speed dial button that connected me to Claude's home.

The conversation was very brief.

"Hey, Max, what's up?"

"Get your ass over here, pronto!"

"You okay?"

"Yeah. Just get over here."

Then I clicked off the phone and pressed the button that connected me to the Sarge's residence.

CHAPTER 51

Claude arrived at my house in less time than seemed possible.

"Where'd you park the Lear jet?" I asked as I let him in.

"Well, being the way that you scared the living shit out of me, I figured that it probably wasn't a real good time to be pretending to be taking my road test. *What the hell is going on, Max?*"

"Follow me."

I led him down the hallway to my answering machine sitting on top of my dresser and pressed the replay button. When the tape started playing, he bent his head down to listen.

When it ended, he looked up at me and said, "Now what the fuck was that all about?"

"My sentiments exactly," I said as Claude followed me back down the hallway to the kitchen.

"Want a beer?" I asked.

"Yeah. Got any chips to go along with it?"

"How is it that I knew that was coming?" I asked as I handed him a large, unopened bag of assorted chips, called Munchies.

He looked at the picture on the bag and said, "Man, these things look *good.*"

Being that Claude is a lot more like family than guest, I didn't bother waiting for him to sit down on the living room sofa, before sitting myself down in my easy chair.

"Did you call the Sarge yet?" Claude asked.

"Yeah, he's checking out the tracer. I'm going to be meeting with him tomorrow morning, unless, of course, he finds a need for us to meet beforehand."

"Do you think that this Lisa Sanchez is starting to play games with you?"

I shrugged my shoulders.

"Well, did it sound anything like her?"

"You heard the tape, Claude. That voice was disguised beyond recognition."

"Well, who the hell else could it have been, if not her?"

"I've got an idea," I said. "How about if *I* start asking the

114

obvious questions and you start answering them?"

"Listen," Claude began, "the voice of the guy who's been calling was distorted, just like this one was, yet you said that it might have sounded familiar. So I guess that would mean that this one probably doesn't. Make sense?"

"Well, yes and no. Yes, because it sounds logical and no, because your point might not be valid."

"I'm listening," Claude said.

"The other voice didn't sound familiar, at first, either. So maybe after I listen to this one enough times, something about it might ring a bell. Who knows?"

"Who knows, is right." Claude said, "That's the stage we're at once again. The 'who the fuck knows' stage."

My partner's rather pessimistic way of summing things up was quite understandable, considering that the case seemed to be moving at a "one step forward, two steps back" pace for quite some time.

But despite this, I personally was beginning to feel a rare sense of optimism. I had a feeling that receiving a phone call from a woman expressing concern about Lisa Sanchez's welfare, on the same day that I ran into Father Stanton in a funeral procession line, meant that the forward steps were finally ready to start making up for lost ground.

CHAPTER 52

The following morning, I was in such a hurry to get to the precinct that I didn't even take the time to stop for my usual cup of coffee. Nor did I go straight to my office, like I usually do when I arrive at the precinct each morning.

Instead, I headed straight to the Sarge's office. He was sitting at his desk, reading the newspaper.

"Neither of yesterday's calls were traceable," he said as I walked into his office.

"No surprise there. I don't think that either of them lasted longer than ten seconds."

"So tell me about Father Stanton."

I sat down before responding.

"Well, he looks as though he could have probably gotten his ass whipped by any one of those little girls. He's no youngster."

"That old, huh?"

"Sixty-eight. But he looks much older. He barely had enough strength to shake my hand."

"You sure he was trying?"

.   I thought about that one for a minute.

"I assumed that he was. Now that I think about it, though, I guess that it's impossible for me to say for certain. But based on what he looked like, his handshake felt appropriate.'

"All that means is that you got what you expected. It doesn't necessarily mean that it was all he was capable of. He could be a lefty, for all you know."

"You're right. That never even crossed my mind."

"Do you think he'll call you?"

"That's what I'm here to discuss with you, Earl. I realize that Dr. Forrester had advised us not to question the guy yet. But I think that the situation has changed because of yesterday. It'll no longer be a surprise visit."

"But since you told him to call you, it would, in essence, be exactly that. What else would you call it?"

"I know what you're saying, Sarge. But I've got this feeling in my gut that it would be a good idea for me to pay him a visit right now."

"Well, I wish we had more to go on than a feeling in your gut."

"Don't you remember this past winter, when that seventeen-year-old kid…."

The Sarge held up his hand to stop me.

"Okay, Max. Since you ran into him yesterday, I'll let you talk with him. But don't turn it into an interrogation! Just try to get a feel for the guy, and if possible, try and get an idea of how well he knows Lisa Sanchez. And be sure to keep your meeting as brief as possible."

"Gotcha, Earl. Thanks."

I stood up and leaned over his desk to shake his hand.

He barely gripped my outstretched hand.

Then he looked up at me and grinned.

Like I said, the Sarge ain't stupid.

CHAPTER 53

He held his tiny binoculars up to his eyes and focused in on his subject.

There she was - Briana, playing with her friends, their mothers sitting on lawn chairs, watching them closely.

"Not today, you idiot!" the voice screamed.

"Shut your mouth!" he muttered.

"As you wish, sissy boy."

It was Mrs. Rodgers' first time at a playground since Briane's abduction. Briana had been playing at her camp's playground on a daily basis, but camp was now over. After much pleading from her daughter, she agreed to join Briana's friends and their moms for early morning playtime at the local schoolyard.

"Don't you know what 'not today' means? You imbecile!" the voice yelled.

"Enough already, you fools."

He knew the voices were right this time. But it made no difference. The twin had become his unyielding obsession. The redhead at Bear Mountain and Tara from her own backyard did little to satisfy him.

His luck ran dry, however, when the mothers folded up their chairs, gathered their daughters together and left the playground.

His act would not be carried out, not this time.

As he walked back to his car, the voices began their taunting.

"Little sissy-boy doesn't listen, does he?"

"Quiet, you idiots," he screamed.

Their unrelenting torment continued as he drove away and headed for the parkway. The closer that he got to his home, the more diminished became the sounds of battle within the mind of the Hangman.

CHAPTER 54

I stopped for a cup of joe at a small corner coffee shop around the block from the school. I was feeling a little out of sorts and I figured that my lack of caffeine was probably the reason.

After I sipped down my second cup, I got up and headed to Thomas Stanton's apartment, which was located within the school that bore his name.

It took him quite a while to come to the door, quite possibly because he could barely hear the ringing of the doorbell.

"Detective Miller, it's good to see you," he said upon opening the door.

I shook his hand, receiving much the same feeble grip as the day before.

"I happened to be in your neck of the woods, Father Stanton, so I figured I'd stop by. I hope you don't mind."

"Not at all. Come on in, please."

I followed him into the living room, to the two chairs nearest the window.

"Can I get you anything, Detective?" he asked.

"No, I'm fine, thanks. Would you mind if I turned the chairs so that we can face each other?" I asked.

"Go right ahead."

After we were seated, I asked, "Do you have any idea as to the whereabouts of Claudia Sanchez?"

"No, I don't. Is she okay?"

"I certainly hope so. What can you tell me about Mrs. Sanchez?"

"Lovely lady, or so she seems."

"Did you know that she moved out of her apartment?"

"No, I didn't. She hasn't returned any of my phone calls. But I had no idea that it was because she had moved."

"Would you happen to know of any man that she was close with? A priest, perhaps?"

"No. I really don't know much about her at all."

"How long was Claudia a student here?"

"She completed her third year this past June."

I hesitated for a moment, then asked, "Do you, by any

119

chance, know a Father Ken Vecchia?"

"Sure, I know Ken. His parish is in Bayside. Why do you ask?"

"Well, Ken's been a friend of mine since childhood."

"Heck of a nice guy."

"Always has been," I replied.

At that point, I had come to the conclusion that Father Stanton either knew nothing about the murders or he was one heck of an outstanding liar. Of course, there are many, many times in police interrogation work where differentiating the two can prove to be a mighty tough task. Nonetheless, I felt that it was the proper time to end the questioning - brief and non-intimidating.

So I stood up and waited for Father Stanton to do the same.

"Thanks for your time, Father. You've got my card if you need me, right?"

"I sure do," he replied.

When we got to the front door, I offered him my left hand this time.

His grip was quite a bit stronger than with his right hand.

CHAPTER 55

After I left the Thomas Stanton School, I decided to stop by Lisa Sanchez's apartment to see if the super had anything new to report.

No one answered when I rang the intercom buzzer of his apartment, so I once again used my shoulder to nudge open the front door. From there, I walked down the long hallway to his apartment and rang his doorbell a few times.

There was no answer.

So I headed up the staircase to Lisa's apartment and tried turning her doorknob. The door was locked, so I rang her doorbell, to no avail.

The scent of brewed coffee was lingering in the hallway. It was coming from the apartment next to Lisa's. I decided to knock on the door, to see what her next-door neighbor had to say about her.

A short, elderly woman came to the door.

I showed her my badge and said, "Good morning, ma'am. I'm Detective Miller, from the Nassau County Police Department."

With a sweet little grin on her face, she said, "Nassau County? I think you made a wrong turn somewhere, Detective."

I returned the grin. There aren't many things more uplifting to me than a nice elderly woman with a sense of humor.

"Care for a cup of coffee?" she asked.

I was about to turn down her offer, but the caffeine fiend in me would have no part of it.

"Sure, if it isn't too much of a bother."

"If it were, then I wouldn't have made the offer."

After she poured the two of us a cup of coffee, I asked, "How well do you know your neighbor, Lisa Sanchez?"

"I might have seen her once or twice. We exchanged "hellos." That was the extent of it."

"Are you aware that she had a young daughter?"

"A daughter? I wonder where she's been hiding her."

"You and me, both," I thought, to myself.

We shot the breeze for a few more minutes, then I thanked

her and headed back to my car.

I ran into the super when I got outside. He had just closed his car door and was heading towards the building.

After we shook hands, he asked, "Any word on Mrs. Sanchez?"

"My question exactly."

"Well, if you do find her, tell her I'm keeping her apartment open for her. I hope she'll be needing it."

"You and me both," I replied.

Then we shook hands and headed in opposite directions.

CHAPTER 56

I headed to the Sarge's office when I arrived back at the precinct. His door was closed. But I heard voices coming from inside, so I gave the door a couple of soft knocks.

"Come in," the Sarge said.

When I opened the door, I caught sight of Penny Forrester, seated on the chair across from him.

"Be with you in two minutes, Max."

So I closed the door and stood in the hallway until the Sarge finally gave me the okay to enter.

"So, how'd it go, Max?" he asked as soon I was seated.

"Well, he said that he knew very little about Lisa Sanchez. Whether I believe him or not, I can't say for certain. But he sure seemed genuine. Oh, by the way, he's a lefty."

The Sarge grinned.

"I stopped by Lisa Sanchez's apartment on the way back," I said.

"And?"

"And nothing. It was a waste of my time."

The Sarge glanced over at Penny Forrester, then looked back at me and said, "Dr. Forrester would like to speak with you, Max. To see if there's anything that you might have overlooked."

"Sure, go right ahead."

"I think it would be best if we spoke in private, Detective," Dr. Forrester said.

Then the Sarge stood up and said, "As I had just finished telling Dr. Forrester, I have a meeting with the Commissioner in a little while. So why don't the two of you move into Detective Miller's office and have your meeting there."

CHAPTER 57

Dr. Forrester started off our conversation at my weak point - the women in my life.

"Are you now or have you recently been in a relationship with a member of the opposite sex?" she asked.

"Yes, there's a young lady that I've been living with for almost two years. I broke it off a little over a week ago."

"What's her name?"

"Kerri. Kerri Bailey."

My face must have surely turned bright red when she asked her next question.

"Do you have any children?"

"Yes, one daughter," I replied.

"What's her name?"

"Jill."

"How old is Jill?"

"She's thirty."

"Are you close with her?"

I was less embarrassed when I pissed in my pants in kindergarten than I was when she asked me that. I realized that this didn't make a whole heck of a lot of sense, being that the person doing the asking was a shrink. I also realized that what I was about to say wouldn't be real high up on her list of the most earth-shattering things that she'd ever heard. But it didn't matter. I still felt like a first-class asshole.

"I haven't spoken with Jill in many years."

"Tell me a little about this woman, Kerri, who you were living with."

The doc was good enough to change the subject when she saw how uncomfortable it was for me to discuss my relationship with Jill. Little did she know, I had other issues, like Kerri.

"What would you like to know?" I asked, hoping that she would again change the subject.

"What does she do for a living?"

"Well, she's in the entertainment industry." *Ah, who was I trying to kid!* "She's a dancer, an exotic dancer."

She thought for a moment, and then said, "So that would obviously put her in close contact with a lot of different men."

"A little *too close* is what I eventually learned."

Then the doc broke the ice, thank God.

"I'm almost afraid to ask, but are there any other women in your life?"

I smiled as my anxiety quickly dissipated.

"Lucky for them, no, there aren't any. Not at the present time, at least."

CHAPTER 58

During the course of our discussion, I learned that, like me, the doc had been married twice before. I learned as well that she also had one daughter. Unlike me, however, she was in close contact with hers.

She eventually turned the conversation back to Kerri, by asking, "Is Kerri a prostitute? Is that what you found out about her?"

"No. I don't think that she's a prostitute. But anything's possible, I guess."

"What hours does she work?"

"Five in the afternoon until two in the morning, except for Thursdays and Sundays."

"How old is she?"

"Twenty-eight…and a half."

We looked at each other and smiled.

Then, all grew silent.

It wasn't an empty silence that fell between us, but rather, one with an unspoken message; a silence that comes before a man and woman embrace for the very first time. There was a big problem with this one, however. She was sitting on the opposite side of the desk from me, which meant that I would have had to stand up and walk around it in order to embrace her. This was way too risky, being that I didn't know for certain if she shared my sentiments. My gut was pretty darn certain that she did, though.

Our unspoken moment eventually ended when she said, "I think it would be a good idea for someone to keep an eye on Kerri Bailey, during her working hours. I'd be curious to know the company she keeps."

CHAPTER 59

Guy Saladino was the Sarge's first choice to go undercover at Time to Unwind. I talked him out of that one rather quickly, however, by reminding him of the little incident that Saladino and I had after he consumed a few drinks too many.

Noodle was a much better candidate anyway. He was overly pale and kind of sleazy looking, thus making him a perfect fit. Saladino was more ordinary looking, which I believe might very well have made him that much more conspicuous. Needless to say, the criteria for what comprised normalcy in this instance were, with no pun intended, a direct deviation from the norm.

I personally felt that Dr. Forrester was going on a bit of a wild goose chase with this one. But as a trained professional in the study of human behavior, maybe she knew better than me.

Noodle came back empty after the first few nights. No one seemed suspicious and nothing seemed out of the ordinary. The fourth night he noticed a guy eyeballing Kerri the entire night. But the guy requested lap dances from just about every dancer in the place, except for Kerri.

Noodle later followed the guy home, to make note of his address.

My partner and I had reached the same conclusions about the guy. He was probably some down-on-his-luck schnook who couldn't approach Kerri because he found her very good looks to be too intimidating. If a guy was lacking in confidence, a woman like Kerri might be more than he could handle, even if it was merely a lap dance that he desired.

The Sarge wasn't taking any chances, though. So he insisted that Claude and I keep an eye on the guy for awhile.

CHAPTER 60

Theodore Rose was the guy's name. He was an actuary at an insurance company. He lived about five miles from his workplace.

He also happened to be married with a couple of kids.

If there was ever a stereotypical suburban husband, this guy was it. He'd leave for work at 8:00 a.m. and return home at 5:30 in the evening every day, like clockwork. He even looked the part - wireless glasses, sporty-looking SUV and all.

The question still remained, what was a guy like this doing at a place like Time to Unwind? A better question, perhaps, was what he was doing there alone. Usually, guys like Rose will frequent places like that with other guys, after a ball game, or an office party, or something along those lines.

Claude hypothesized that the guy probably had a little spat with his wife, stormed out of the house and ended up there.

"But why is it that he didn't request a lap dance from the one woman that he was watching all night?" I inquired of my partner.

"Well, like we had said yesterday, he probably found Kerri too intimidating."

"I don't know about that one anymore Claude. If he were a single guy who was deathly afraid of women, yeah. But a married guy I'm not so sure about. He does, after all, have two kids, so he had to have gotten laid a couple of times, at least. I was thinking more along the lines of a middle-aged guy whose mother's lips were the only ones that he'd ever kissed."

"Hey Max, you're the one that didn't even know that his stripper girlfriend was also a lap dancer. And now, all of a sudden, you're an authority on the subject?"

Then, as if it were someone else doing the talking, I heard myself say, "Why don't we meet with Penny Forrester and discuss it with her."

"Good idea," Claude replied.

CHAPTER 61

The morning of our scheduled meeting with Penny Forrester, I made a suggestion to Claude.

"Hey, Claude," I said, "I think that we'd probably be better off if you check to see what Rose is up to while I meet with Dr. Forrester. I really don't see the need for the two of us to meet with her while no one's watching Rose."

"Did you say that we'd be better off, or that you'd be better off?"

I played dumb.

"I don't get ya."

"Max, if you'd like to be alone with the lady, why don't you just tell me so?"

After eleven years, the guy knows me almost as well as I know myself, and there I was, trying to pull the wool over his eyes.

"Anyway, you're right, one of us should be keeping an eye on him and I hereby volunteer for that assignment."

So off he went.

The doctor arrived at my office at eleven-fifty, ten minutes ahead of schedule. Before she even had a chance to sit down, I asked, "Are you hungry?"

She glanced down at her watch and said, "I'm getting there."

"It's a bit of a drive, but I know of this great Italian restaurant in Amityville. If you're interested, that is."

"Sure. Why not?" she replied.

So, off we went.

"Want the top up or down?" I asked as I opened the car door for her.

She stood there thinking it over and then said, "Ah, what the heck, let's go topless."

Neither of us said a word during our twenty-minute ride to Amityville. Instead, we gave an occasional smile to one another to let each other know that we were enjoying our "wind in our faces" drive.

Amityville is a quaint little waterfront village in the southwesternmost part of Suffolk County. Its name is more familiar-sounding to most when it precedes the word "horror."

This can be justly blamed on a couple of grade-B movies which, as I've been told, are filled with about as much sincerity as that which comes out of a professional wrestler's mouth while he's promoting his next fight.

Amato's is a romantic little Italian restaurant in the southern section of the village. Its superb fifty-dollar soup-to-nuts dinner can be had for about fifteen during weekday lunch hours.

When we arrived there, I requested a booth in the downstairs dining area, handing the immaculately dressed maître d' a five spot while doing so.

The lower level is a whole lot cozier than the upper.

I waited for Penny to sit, then sat down next to her.

We sat there, studying our menus. Then I placed mine down and asked her, "Do you know what you want?"

She turned to look at me.

Then, it happened. We embraced each other and kissed.

"I hardly even know you, yet I feel so darn comfortable talking with you," Penny whispered in my ear.

"I knew that you could fix minds, but I didn't know that you could read them as well," I whispered into hers.

Like a couple of overaged adolescents, we resumed our public display of affection.

CHAPTER 62

It's a good thing that I live only about five minutes from the restaurant. Otherwise, the headlines of the evening edition of the New York Post might have read something like, "Cop and Shrink in Hangman Case Caught With Their Pants Down."

My poor beloved canine, Sparky, almost got himself trampled in the process. He didn't know better than to not be sleeping in a hallway which two mammals in heat had to pass through in order to gain access to a bedroom.

Penny Forrester, I was quite pleased to discover, was every bit as competent a lover as she was a psychiatrist. She made that fifteen-dollar soup-to-nuts lunch at Amato's well worth skipping. Coming from a glutton like myself, that's saying a lot.

Afterwards, as we lay there elated and exhausted, I picked up the phone and called Claude on his cell phone.

He answered on the first ring.

"Listen, partner, I'm taking a half mental health day. Think you'll be okay without me?"

"Jesus, I don't know, Max. What if Rose does something crazy, like scratching his balls?"

When I was composed enough to speak, I said, "Sorry, partner, you're on your own."

Penny had a real good laugh as well when I told her of Claude's perceived dilemma.

My call to Claude precipitated the reason that Penny and I were supposed to get together in the first place - to discuss Theodore Rose.

I told her of how Noodle spotted him eying Kerri all night, and everything else that went along with the story.

Without even pausing to think it over, she said, "Let me ask you this, Max. How often do you find yourself lying in bed with a naked woman beside you when you're supposed to be at work?"

"That's an easy one. Just about never."

"So I wouldn't be correct if I were to draw the conclusion that Max Miller sneaks home in the middle of the day to fool around? Would I?"

"I know what you're saying. A guy sneaking off to a strip

joint for a night is not a big deal. But what about his obsession with Kerri and the way Noodle said he was eyeballing her all night?"

She smiled and said, "Well, you've been eyeballing me for quite some time now."

"I didn't think you noticed."

"I sure did. Not that I'm complaining about it."

"So I take it that you don't think Theodore Rose is the guy."

"Based on what you've told me, I very seriously doubt it. So does your partner, apparently."

"Now whatever gave you that idea?"

We shared a few giggles. Then I crossed my fingers, held them out in front of me and said, "Are you doing anything Saturday night?"

Without saying a word, she grabbed hold of my fingers and slowly put them into her mouth, performing on them what she had earlier performed on another part of my anatomy.

Then she looked into my eyes and said, "I am doing something Saturday night. Want to know what?"

I nodded my head.

"Anything you want me to."

Her seductive words sent a warm rush through my body. Taking notice of its effect, she gently sat herself on top.

Round two had officially begun.

CHAPTER 63

Despite the fact that we were ready to leave for my office with plenty of time to spare, I still arrived a half an hour late for work the next morning. It seems that the doc and I had a real hard time making it out my front door. Our problem stemmed from the fact that after we got dressed, neither of us was too keen on the idea of staying that way.

As I was walking into the precinct, after watching Penny drive her silver Lexus SUV out of the parking lot, I was feeling so darn good that I actually caught myself whistling "Zip-a-Dee-Doo-Dah." Being that I couldn't recall having whistled anything since I was a kid, I found this to be quite amusing. With my luck being what it is, Claude and the Sarge happened to be standing in the hallway chatting at the same time that I walked into the precinct, chuckling to myself.

"Do you want to let us in on it, or do you prefer to be alone when you laugh?" my partner shouted from down the hallway.

"Private joke, you guys wouldn't get it," I shouted back.

"You keeping bankers' hours, Max?" the Sarge asked as I approached.

"Sorry, Sarge, I had a hard time getting out of bed this morning."

The Sarge glanced over at Claude, then looked at me and said, "I wonder why."

It was now their turn to laugh, and that they did, but good. After watching the two of them carry on for long enough, I said, "You know, you guys are beginning to remind me of Beavis and Butthead, the way that you're standing there, giggling like two-year-olds."

A little while later, as I sat in my office with my feet upon my desk, I was still feeling as high as a kite. But then, all of a sudden, the guilt overtook me with the same suddenness and headstrong determination as my last stomach virus.

I felt as though I had no right to feel the way that I did until I caught him. No right to feel joy until I rid the playgrounds of the dead silence of funeral homes. No right to feel contentment until I transformed little girls' nightmares back into sweet, peaceful dreams. No right to feel anything, except the pain that those poor, defenseless little girls were forced to feel.

CHAPTER 64

An hour or so after we had parted company in the hallway, the Sarge buzzed me on the intercom.

"What are you doing, Max?" he asked.

"At the present time? Not a whole heck of a lot."

"Well, in that case, come over to my office. There's something that I need to discuss with you."

After I sat down in the uncomfortable steel-framed chair across from him, the Sarge said, "Perhaps it's none of my business, Max, but I'm wondering where things stand between you and Dr. Forrester."

To almost anyone else who may have been sitting in the Sarge's chair at the time, I would have said something to the effect of, "You're right, it is none of your business." But I knew the Sarge well enough to know that he wouldn't be asking such a question because he was being nosy.

"Well, it's kind of hard to say at this point, Earl. We barely even know each other. But the chemistry is there, no doubt about it."

The Sarge caught me off guard with what he said next.

"She's a good woman, Max. I think she'll be real good for you. I honestly do."

I couldn't stop the smile from spreading across my face.

"I think you're right, Sarge. But time will tell, I guess."

The Sarge returned my smile, but an instant later, his face became blank.

"That's not the reason that I called you in here, Max. Not that I didn't mean what I just said."

Man, the Sarge was sure beating around the bush. Sergeant Earl usually gets right to the point - one, two, three.

"This is going to be my last week, Max. I'm retiring. That's what my meeting with the Commissioner was all about the other day."

I sat there in shock, totally and completely dumbfounded.

The Sarge must have noticed how taken back I was because he took a long pause before he continued speaking.

"He asked me who I'd recommend to fill my spot. There was nothing to think about. You're the one, Max."

"I'm deeply honored, Sarge. Thank you."

"I'm sure you're wondering why I decided to leave in the middle of the case."

I nodded my head.

"Since Betsy died, things haven't been the same for me, Max."

Betsy was the Sarge's wife of forty-eight years. She had died quite unexpectedly, in her sleep, a little less than a year prior.

"I was hoping that this case would give me some relief from thinking about her so much. It's done just the opposite. Every little girl's death brought me back to how I felt the day that she died. I figured that catching the guy would bring some closure to Betsy. It might have, but from the looks of things..."

"I'm gonna catch him, Sarge. For the sake of those poor little girls, I'm gonna catch him. And for the sake of my sanity as well."

"That's why I brought up you and Penny. I don't want this case to stand in the way. Don't deprive yourself like I have, Max. Don't let the guilt control you. All that does is give this fucking creep another victory."

CHAPTER 65

Penny's home was located in Setauket, an upper-class village on the north shore of Suffolk County. She lived in a ranch-style house that appeared to be twice the size of mine.

I almost didn't recognize her when she opened the front door. Her lips were covered in dark red lipstick and she was wearing more makeup than usual. A black, lightweight dress clung seductively against her thin, curvaceous figure.

"My God, you look so beautiful," I said as I handed her a bouquet of flowers.

"Why, thank you. Now, please don't let my looks intimidate you, Sergeant Miller."

"Why, you give lap dances, too?"

"For you? Anytime!"

We kissed, for what I wished could have been forever, as we stood there with her front door wide open.

"Come on, I'll show you around," she said as she closed the door and grabbed hold of my hand.

She led me around the bend and into her den. Despite its contemporary décor, it had a warm, cozy feel to it.

Then, she led me to her bedroom.

She flicked on the light to give me a chance to peek inside. Then she flicked it off and said, "That one you'll get a better look at later."

Our tour abruptly ended in the dining room, where the table was set for two. She placed the bouquet of flowers inside a tall glass of water and then placed it down in the center of the table.

"I whipped up some surf and turf - filet mignon and lobster tails. Hope you don't mind."

Penny's cooking turned out to be out of this world. I couldn't help myself from complimenting her on it every two minutes.

When the main course was eaten, or in my case devoured, Penny said, "Want to guess what I made for dessert?"

Having sipped away my inhibitions with the three glasses of wine that accompanied the delectable cuisine, I got up and stood behind her. Then I gently unzipped her dress and began fondling her.

I lowered my head and whispered in her ear, "Want to guess what I want?"

Unlike the lunch at Amato's that we had also decided to pass up, those two cups of chocolate mousse didn't go uneaten. Penny snuck into the kitchen later that night, and brought them into the bedroom.

They were a perfect nightcap to a scrumptious dessert.

CHAPTER 66

"Where are ya off to?" I asked upon being awakened by the feel of Penny's soft lips on my unshaven face.

"I've got a meeting at the school at eight. It should take no more than an hour, so don't go anywhere."

"Who the hell schedules a meeting at 8:00 on a Sunday morning?"

"Ah, some asshole," she whispered as she bent back down to kiss my cheek before heading out the bedroom door.

A little while later, I decided to make certain that the link between my answering machine and cell phone was working properly. So I grabbed Penny's phone from atop her night table and called my home.

As I often do upon hearing the sound of my voice on the other end of the line, I began to visualize my answering machine sitting atop my dresser.

Then I realized something. Father Stanton had told me that Lisa Sanchez hadn't returned any of his phone calls. Big problem there - she took her answering machine with her when she left. I had made note of that fact when Claude and I were in her apartment because it was sitting on the ledge of her kitchenette the first time that I was there. It was one of those telephone-and-answering-machines combined into one. But it wasn't there when Claude and I went there on the day that she moved out. I didn't see it in her bedroom, either.

So, with the adrenaline now in control, I shot out of bed and got dressed in a flash.

On my way out the front door, I stopped by the kitchen and tried to find a pen and a sheet of paper so that I could write Penny a note. I found a pen in one of the drawers, but I couldn't find a piece of paper anywhere. So on one of the white paper plates that she kept in that same drawer, I wrote, "Penny, I'll call you later - something real big has come up."

Then came the hard part: trying to figure out how to sign off. I couldn't just write "Max" because that would appear a bit cold. Then it came to me. My mom would always sign notes that she'd leave for my siblings and me as "L, Mom." In my mom's case, "L" was an abbreviation. In this case, it was just the beginning of a four-letter word, one which I've never exactly been accused of overusing.

CHAPTER 67

Claude insisted that my early Sunday morning phone call didn't wake him.

"No, I was up. I was up."

"Sure you were, Claude."

My partner was so tired that he almost sounded drunk. Until, that is, I told him about my latest observation.

"Holy shit, Max! Holy shit! A break, a break in this fucking case! Where are you? Get your ass over here. Where are you?"

If I had to bet on it, I'd say that Claude drove himself to tears while he was yelling that. That's how excited he sounded. He'd never admit it, but I could hear it in his voice. Not that I'm knocking it or anything like that, I mean, after my Judy Garland performance at Tara's funeral, it would certainly be hypocritical of me, at the very least. To say that the case was taking an emotional toll on the two of us would be putting it very mildly.

"I just left Penny's house in Setauket."

"How about if you meet me at the school? I can get there a lot sooner than you can get here."

"What's the rush, Claude? He's not going anywhere."

"How do you know?"

"Because either he wouldn't have come back from overseas or else he would have taken off by now. Believe me."

"But why even take the chance?"

Claude was right.

"I'll tell you what, Claude, go there and sit in front of the place. If you see him leave, then follow him. Otherwise wait in your car until I get there."

"Gotcha."

Under normal circumstances, I would have had no problem with Claude going it alone. I never have, for that matter. The term "normal circumstances," however, had become a foreign phrase to us.

CHAPTER 68

Claude was sitting in his parked car in front of the school when I got there. I pulled up behind him and grabbed my "Police Business" sign out of the glove compartment and placed it on top of the dashboard.

"Anything going on?" I asked.

"Not out here, there isn't."

When we got to the entranceway of the building, I rang Father Stanton's intercom button a couple of dozen times. There was no answer. Being that it was Sunday morning and that he was a clergyman, we surmised that he was at Sunday mass. We were probably too wound up to figure that one out earlier. So we left the building and walked the few blocks to the coffee shop, figuring that we'd check back a little while later.

When we arrived there, I grabbed a copy of the Sunday New York Times and Claude took a copy of Newsday from the stacks of papers that were piled up in front of the place. Then we walked over to the counter and sat down.

The waitress who was working the counter was a lot younger and a whole heck of a lot prettier than the one who had served me the last time.

When I was finished checking out the box score of the previous night's Yankee game, I pulled out the main section of the paper. A photograph in the lower right corner of page one caught my eye immediately. It was of an empty playground. The swings in the photo were dangling in the wind. Below it, read, "Playgrounds on Long Island, like this one at Eisenhower Park in East Meadow, sit unoccupied."

I lifted up the paper for Claude to see and said, "I wonder what our friends in the Big Apple have to say this time."

While I was reading through the article, the waitress came over and poured me some more coffee. She caught sight of what I was reading.

With her wad of gum popping as she spoke, she said, "Think they'll ever catch the guy?"

I looked up and said, "I'm sure they will."

While still chomping away on her gum, she replied, "Until they do, I'm never gonna bring a kid into this world. I don't want no daughter of mine having to fear for her life all the time. That's no way for a kid to have to live."

For lack of a more intelligent response, I said, "Maybe you'll have a son. Who knows?"

She shook her head, then turned around and walked back into the kitchen.

The very second that I saw Claude put the last morsel of food into his mouth, I stood up and said, "Come on, let's get out of here. That gum popping is starting to get to me."

"Yeah, I know what you mean," Claude said.

I pulled out my wallet and laid a twenty on the counter to cover the cost of our newspapers and breakfasts.

"That's a pretty generous tip that you're leaving her, considering the way that she was popping her gum in our faces," Claude said.

One thing that he's not is naïve. Thus I'm certain that Claude knew quite well that the young lady's chewing habits had nothing at all to do with us wanting to get our fat asses back to work in such a hurry.

CHAPTER 69

No one buzzed us in to grant us entry to the school, so we tried to jimmy the door open. The dead bolt on the inside, though, proved to make that a virtual impossibility.

After waiting in vain for someone to enter or leave the building, we decided to take off. We reached the conclusion that the late afternoon, after all of the church services were over, would be a better time to stop by.

Claude suggested that we take a ride to North Shore University Hospital, where Lisa Sanchez used to work. When I reminded him that Noodle and Saladino had already been there on a couple of occasions, he responded with those all too familiar words.

"We've got nothing to lose."

When we arrived at the huge hospital complex, Claude parked his Ford Explorer next to the main entrance. Just as I stepped out, Penny called me on my cell phone. I proceeded to tell her of my reason for scooting out of her house the way that I did. To this, she replied, "That was a very impressive use of your analytical skills, Sergeant Miller."

Then she asked me what the "L" on the paper plate stood for.

Even though I was pretty sure that she was putting me on, I played it safe by telling her that it stood for "Lieutenant, which comes right after the rank of Sergeant."

At the end of our conversation, we exchanged rather mushy goodbyes.

"How come you never talk like that to me?" my wise-ass partner asked after I clicked off my phone.

"Sorry Claude, but you oversized African-American guys just don't do it for me."

Out came Claude's effeminate voice. "Well, if that's the case, then I don't know if I want to be your partner any longer."

We stopped dead in our tracks. In that very instant, the shock of it had, finally, hit us. Our partnership was about to end. What a partnership it had been. The Claude Greer and Max Miller partnership was like that of two soldiers who shared a foxhole and fought on the front line together for eleven years.

144

I wasn't as pained by the thought of our upcoming breakup as I might have imagined. The fact that Claude would now be my right-hand man, and that his office would be just down the hall from mine, helped ease the pain, no doubt. What made it easiest to bear, however, was the fact that a new partnership was developing in my life - one that brought with it a different kind of pain. The kind that I could feel in the pit of my stomach, from those damn butterflies.

CHAPTER 70

Florence McDermott, the head of housekeeping, was a rather large-sized woman of African-American descent with a bright, uplifting smile that seemed to never want to leave her. Her office, though not large and void of any windows, had a certain look of distinction to it. Its plush, green carpet and wood-paneled walls probably had a lot to do with it.

Ms. McDermott told us much the same as she had told Noodle and Saladino previously. Lisa Sanchez was a rather quiet young lady who did her job well and was rarely absent or tardy. She had nothing but positive things to say about her. It didn't take us long to realize that she wasn't going to be of any help to us. So we asked to speak with the woman that our colleagues had spoken with, a Helen Floss. She, as Noodle had informed us, was the co-worker with whom Lisa had been closest.

When she arrived, Ms. McDermott bid us a cordial farewell and then quietly closed the door behind her.

Helen Floss was a petite young lady, with Irish green eyes and short, jet-black hair. She sat down behind her boss's desk, at our request.

"You look pretty comfortable, sitting there," I said to break the ice.

She smiled.

"Maybe, one day," She replied.

"I guess you know why we're here," Claude said.

"Yes, I do. I'm glad that you picked this Sunday to come here. I only work one Sunday a month."

"We realize that you have already spoken with Detectives McCorry and Saladino. We're here to find out if you have anything new to tell, something that might have come up since your meeting with them," I said.

She hesitated for a moment and then said, "After the gentlemen were here the last time I thought of something that I had forgotten to tell them. The trouble is, I can't remember what it was."

Claude and I exchanged quick glances. The kind with "oy vey" written all over them.

146

"We know that Lisa had spoken to you about the dreams that she'd been having. Can you tell us a little about that?" my partner asked.

"Well, like I had told the other gentlemen, she said that she'd been dreaming about some guy that she thought was the killer."

Tears began to form in her eyes. She used the white sleeve of her uniform to wipe them away.

"I wish that she would have told me more about what was going on in her life. She was such, she *is,* such a nice person and such a beautiful, beautiful woman. I told her that she missed her calling, she should have been a model. Deep down, I knew that it wouldn't have been for her, though. She was way too private a person. The publicity would have driven her crazy."

"Did she tell you anything about what the man looked like?" I asked.

"No. She shrugged it off. She'd tell me that it wasn't important, that it was only a dream."

Then I stood up, thanked her for her time and handed her one of my cards.

On her way out the door, she turned back around to look at us.

"It's stuck there, in the back of my mind, but I still can't remember what it is."

"Well you've got my card, if you do," I replied.

CHAPTER 71

No more than ten minutes after we pulled away from the hospital, Ms. Floss called me on my cell phone.

"Detective Miller, I just remembered what it was that I had forgotten to tell the other gentlemen. I thought about it right after they left but then forgot what it was."

If she were one of my siblings, I would have told her to get to the damn point already. But she wasn't, so I very politely said, "I'm most anxious to hear what you have to say."

"When they asked if there were any other co-workers that she might have spoken with about the dreams, I neglected to tell them something because it didn't cross my mind at the time."

It's no wonder that Lisa Sanchez didn't tell her anything. She probably never got the opportunity to get a word in edge-wise.

"The only time that I really got a chance to speak with Lisa during the work day was first thing in the morning and during lunch."

I was good and ready to click off the phone if she didn't get to the point real soon.

"Us housekeepers have a lot more contact with the nurses on our shift than we have with each other."

"How many nurses did she have had contact with?"

"A lot. They shift us around each week. I don't know why, but that's how it is. One week we'll be in cardiac, the next week it could be maternity or orthopedics. But I do remember her telling me about this one nurse that she developed a pretty close friendship with. Unfortunately, I can't for the life of me remember which nurse it was."

"Well, do you know if she discussed the dreams with this person?"

"No, I don't, Detective. I just know that she'd become rather friendly with her."

After I clicked off the phone, Claude asked, "So what did she have to say?"

"She said that Lisa had a lot of contact with the nurses on her shift and that she was close with one nurse in particular.

148

But, of course, she can't remember which one it was."

Claude glanced over at me and then looked back at the road ahead.

"Maybe she did have something to say after all."

"Maybe," I replied, with a shrug of my shoulders.

CHAPTER 72

Claude found a parking spot about a half a block away from the school, or so he thought. It turned out to be a bit too tight a fit for his SUV.

"Were you pretending to be taking your road test, partner?" I kidded as he pulled out of the spot.

"No more partner, Max, not after today. By the way, who's my new partner gonna be?"

"I'm not sure. I was thinking along the lines of some obese, cranky guy who smells like a locker room. How's that sound?"

"Compared to what I've got now, it sounds like a major improvement."

We shared a couple of giggles and then headed to the entrance of the building.

When we got to Father Stanton's apartment, we noticed a note Scotch-taped to his door. Written upon it was, "I'll be in the main office."

So down the hall we went.

As we walked past the staircase, we could see Father Stanton sitting at the front desk.

He offered us a seat when we entered the room.

Claude sat himself down on the chair directly across from him. I, on the other hand, told him that I preferred to stand.

"Father Stanton, the last time that I was here, you mentioned to me that Ms. Sanchez hadn't returned any of your phone calls," I said.

"Yes, that's correct," he replied.

I kept my eyes glued to his as I continued.

"My partner and I don't seem to recall having seen an answering machine in her apartment when we where there on the day that she moved out. And every time we called her number, the phone just kept ringing. No answering machine ever came on."

"That's odd," he said.

"I'd say it is," my fat-assed partner replied.

There you have it - the very reason that I didn't want him going it alone.

Father Stanton opened the bottom drawer of the desk and pulled out a few sheets of white unlined paper which were stapled together. He turned the page and then hit the speakerphone button on the dark green telephone in front of him.

Then he started dialing.

I damn near shit in my pants when I heard the sound of the voice on the other end of the line.

"Hi, this is Lisa. Please leave a message at the beep and I'll call you back."

Claude shot out of his chair and turned around to face me. We were both absolutely speechless.

"I think that I owe you an apology for what I said. I seem to have been jumping to conclusions," Claude said.

"You sure were," I said, to put an exclamation point on Claude's apology.

"Could I take a look at those papers?" I asked.

Father Stanton reached forward and handed them to me.

They contained a listing of the parents' addresses and telephone numbers. So I glanced down the list until I found her name. The address was correct, but the phone number was different than the one that she had given me. I had it memorized ever since I had called her from the golf course that day. The same golf course that, incidentally, I hadn't played on in almost a month.

"Mind if I use your phone?"

After he gave his nod of approval, I phoned Noodle at the precinct and told him the situation. He said that he'd get right to work on tracking down the number. Having never been given reason to doubt Noodle's capability, I knew that the matter was in good hands. If it were his partner with whom I had just spoken, I wouldn't have been so sure.

Sure enough, Noodle called back in no time. He told me that the phone number was unlisted, but was registered in Lisa's name. It was her cell phone number. He also told me that the location where her cell phone had just rung, according to the phone company, was in Flushing, NY.

That's where her apartment is located.

CHAPTER 73

Claude performed his usual array of "Speed Racer" driving techniques, enabling us to arrive at Lisa Sanchez's apartment in no time flat.

I hit the buzzer of the super's apartment to gain entry to the building but received no response. So I gave Claude the honors of budging open the front door.

As we ran up the stairs, we stuck our heads out of the stairwell door on each floor that we came to, in order to see if the super was anywhere in sight. We needed him to gain access to the apartment. He was nowhere to be found, so when we got to her apartment, I started ringing her doorbell, to no avail.

"You really think that she's home?" Claude asked, with a strong emphasis on the sarcasm.

"Did I really think that her voice mail was going to come on, Detective?"

"That's a good point, Sergeant."

"You've got the honors, Detective," I said as I motioned to the door.

Claude grinned.

"Who said my high school football days are behind me?"

Then he bent down into his football stance, and plowed his left shoulder into the door.

It did not at all surprise me to see the door fly open. What did surprise me, however, was that Claude's three hundred and fifty-pound collision didn't cause the walls to come tumbling down around us.

"Are you all right?" I asked.

Out came that infamous Claude Greer smile.

"I think that you should be addressing your question to the door."

I stood there, pretending to be dumbfounded.

"It's amazing how the door opened all by itself, just like that," I said, making obvious reference to our unwarranted form of entry.

I headed straight to the kitchen. Claude went to check the bedroom.

No more than a minute or two later, I heard him shout, "Hey Max, look what I found."

I walked over to the bedroom. Claude was standing there with a cell phone in his hand.

"Where the hell did you find that?"

"Top shelf of the closet, way in the back."

"That's an awfully strange place to keep a cell phone handy. Wait a second, you didn't look up there the first time?"

"I guess not."

As we walked out of the room, Claude pointed at the bottom of the bedroom door and said, "Looks like the super found some time to plaster up the door."

"At least somebody's keeping on top of things," I replied.

Claude gave a little, apologetic shrug of the shoulders. Then we headed for the door.

When we got back to the precinct, Lauren, the switchboard operator, showed us how to retrieve the messages from Lisa's cell phone. There were three messages on it, all from Father Stanton.

CHAPTER 74

The Sarge called me at home, at a little past nine that same night.

He told me that he was calling to wish me good luck in my new position. After I thanked him, he said, "Promise me that you'll catch him, Max."

That seemed like an awfully unusual request coming from the mouth of Sergeant Earl Monahan. But I figured, hey, what the heck. So I said, "I'm going to get him, Sarge. I promise."

"Take care of yourself, Max."

Then, while lying on the same bed that he and Betsy had shared for forty-eight years, he proceeded to blow his brains out.

I haven't been the same person since that night. I never will be, either. When you lose someone that you so admired, you're never the same afterwards. The Sarge knew that better than anyone.

As I watched his casket being lowered into the ground a few days later, I felt neither the sorrow nor the despair that I did during Tara Shiver's burial. My feelings were far more disturbing this time. I was seething with anger. I don't think that I've ever been as infuriated at anyone in my entire life as I was with the Sarge that day. Then the guilt set in, for being so incensed at someone who must have been suffering so terribly. This only fueled my anger.

I was so distraught that I downed a couple of sleeping pills that night. I just wanted to sleep, so I didn't have to think about anything.

With the frame of mind that I was in, I'm damn thankful that I didn't down the entire vial.

CHAPTER 75

When I sat down at the Sarge's desk on the morning after his funeral, I felt as if I, too, had been buried in his casket. It was a feeling that I never again would care to experience, one that emitted a dark and unyielding sense of nothingness.

Following in the Sarge's footsteps was going to be a tough enough task as it was. Following in the footsteps of that same man, now housed six feet beneath the living world with a self-inflicted bullet lodged inside his head, seemed nothing short of torturous - torture that felt as though that bullet in his brain had somehow ricocheted into mine.

That evening, as Penny and I sat at my kitchen table, she asked me a question. One that she undoubtedly knew would stop me from fixating on the loss of my beloved mentor.

"Max," she began in a slow, soft voice, which caused me to turn my focus away from my bowl of wonton soup and into her soft green eyes, "where was it that you told me Jill and her mother had moved to after the divorce?"

As she asked me that, she looked as though she wanted to smile and cry in the same instant, as if she could somehow feel the impact of her words upon my mind.

I looked back down as I gave my reply, not wanting her to see the pain on my face as I spoke.

"Jill's mom, Maureen, moved back to Buffalo with her. That's where she was from and where her family lived. The judge went along with the move because she told him that she needed to live with her parents in order to make ends meet. She was full of crap. It was only an excuse to take Jill as far away from me as possible."

Penny started to say something but I cut her off because talking about Jill made me feel so darn good that I didn't want to stop.

"Jill slowly began to fade from my thoughts, though not from my conscience, by any means. Whenever I'd see a young girl, I'd think about her. Over time, though, I began to block her out of my mind completely. It was the only way that I could deal with the situation without losing my sanity.

"Then the killings began. They brought me back in time. I

would think about her more and more. I would sit home some nights when they first began and look at the pictures that I still have of her for hours at a time. Briane Rodgers' murder was the most difficult one for me because she bore a striking resemblance to Jill."

The conversation got put on hold for a minute or so as we took a few more sips from our soup bowls.

"I think that much of the anger that you're feeling about Earl's suicide has a lot to do with Jill. The guilt as well. You harbor a lot of anger and resentment towards her mother for taking her so far away, and you feel tremendous guilt for not having been there for her. Your feelings of helplessness over that situation were elevated by not being able to help Earl. That's on top of the guilt that you feel over not being able to catch the killer."

I faked a smile and said, "I do appreciate the free psychotherapy, Dr. Forrester."

"Well, that's one of the perks that goes along with dating a shrink."

"You stand to lose a fortune with a guy like me."

"Max?" she said, in the same cautious tone as before. "I think that now is a real good time for us to try and locate Jill."

"Well, as you know, that's my intention, to reunite with her. But do you think it would be a good idea at this particular time?"

"When you catch this son of a bitch, Max, you're going to feel real good, like you're on top of the world. When that feeling fades, however, I think that you're going to want to reunite with Jill more than ever. The void in your life that's been haunting you isn't going to leave you until you find her. So how about if I begin the process of trying to track her down while you concentrate on the case?"

"Do you really think that we'll be able to find her?"

With a slight nod of her head, she said, "I think so."

CHAPTER 76

The next morning, I sat behind the desk once belonging to the late Sergeant Earl Monahan with enough strength to finally face the reality of the situation. The Sarge was gone and what was once his office was now mine. With that came the realization that aside from the unobstructed view of the parking lot which I now had, my new office was the spitting image of my old one. Same drab furnishings, same pale green walls, same pair of oversized shoes resting on the edge of my desk, with Claude Greer's feet sitting inside of them.

"You look like you've come back from the dead, Sergeant Miller," Claude said as he sat there across from me.

"A little psychotherapy á la wonton soup proved to be the cure."

"The Sarge was a great man, Max. You and I both know that. But it's time for us to move on. We've got a maniac to catch."

"Tomorrow's the three-week anniversary of Tara Shiver's murder. Ten days was the longest that he waited prior to this," I said.

"Good news at last," Claude responded.

"Maybe not."

"What's that supposed to mean?" Claude asked, looking as perplexed as he sounded.

I sat there gathering my thoughts before responding.

"Obviously, I'm greatly relieved that he hasn't struck since Tara's murder. But what goes along with that sense of relief is one of concern."

"Yeah. I'm still listening," Claude said, making no attempt to disguise his impatience.

"I've got a strong feeling that he's planning something real big for his next time around."

"What do you think he's got up his sleeve?"

"If I could answer that one, I'd have caught the son of a bitch by now."

"So what makes you say so?"

"I think that things might be getting too easy for him. He might need something more challenging to get his juices flowing."

"More challenging? Man, that's something that I don't even want to think about."

"Well, not thinking about it sure won't help the situation any. Take it from one who knows."

CHAPTER 77

Void of any trace of moonlight, the pitch-black sky above reflected an hour more reminiscent of midnight than the 8:58 p.m. which glowed in red fluorescence from the dashboard in front of him. As he cruised down the dimly lit road, he struggled to remain focused on the act in progress. The force that dictated his thoughts, however, chose to take him elsewhere.

He could feel his grip on the steering wheel begin to tighten as his mind flashed back to the first time that he had met the man.

"Fucking lying hypocrite," he muttered through clenched teeth.

Unlike most of the other runaways that he'd met on the streets of Manhattan, he had managed to get by without having to sell himself to strangers. The messenger job that he had landed afforded him the luxury of a room in a seedy hotel and food, enough to survive.

As time went by, the voices would grow lower in volume and less frequent in occurrence. His independence from his stepfather became a sanctuary to his tormented psyche.

But when he lost his messenger job, desperation began to set in.

Soon thereafter, through what he thought to be fate, he met the clergyman who would take him under his wing. He trusted this man more than he'd ever trusted anyone. He thought him to be his savior.

He learned in time, however, how blind his trust had proven to be.

"Snap out of it, sissy boy, we've got work to do!" the voice shouted as he sat, frozen, in his parked car.

Adhering to its demand, he reached over and pulled the black ski mask out of the brown canvas bag that lay on the passenger seat. He shoved it deep into the pocket of his sweat pants, then flung the door open and stepped out of his jet-black Honda.

He bent down to tie the laces of his black running shoes.

159

Then, he stood up and slammed the door shut. As he lifted up the door handle to make sure that it was locked, he glanced around at the strip mall in front of him.

Then he let go of the handle and began his stroll through the brightly lit parking lot. When he got to the end of the lot, he veered to his left, towards the neighborhood that lay a stone's throw ahead.

Then he began his jog.

In the middle of the quiet, unpretentious piece of suburbia to which he was headed sat the immaculately kept Cape Cod where Briana Rodgers lay in bed, fast asleep with her arms tightly wrapped around her beloved Mr. Teddy.

"Beddy-bye time it will be, my child."

CHAPTER 78

He paid no attention to the small, neatly kept homes as he jogged ahead. Nor did he care to eyeball those select few abodes that were in need of some tender loving care, having neither the time nor the desire to give them his usual quick study.

When he jogged past the point that he had estimated to be his halfway mark, he wiped away the beads of sweat that had gathered on his forehead. Without slowing down, he glanced at his watch.

"Damn it!" he muttered.

Although he was almost ten minutes behind schedule, the voices held back from chastising him for his tardiness. They were well aware that it was their own doings that had caused him to remain seated in his parked car for so long.

After hopping over the white picket fence and landing in the rear yard of his destination, he crept until he was hidden behind a thick, neatly manicured row of bushes.

He sat there, motionless, his eyes glued to the bedroom window of the grief-stricken parents of the late Briane Rodgers.

When their bedroom light no longer shone, Briana's turn would come at last.

CHAPTER 79

A bond, unparalleled by any other, can often develop between identical twins. One so strong that, in certain instances, one sibling may find it difficult to differentiate their own self from the other. On this night, no one was more aware of this sense of shared identity than the twin sister of the late Briane Rodgers.

The dream had frightened Briana terribly. So much so that she refused to believe that it was not she who died on that day, that it was not her own body that lay buried beneath the earth.

"It was me! It was me!" she chanted nonstop, despite her parents' reassurances.

Her anxiety heightened so that her parents contemplated taking her to the emergency room. Upon hearing them talk of this, Briana began to simmer herself down. Being taken to the hospital was almost as frightening to her as the dream itself.

Briana's therapist had voiced opposition to the Rodgers allowing their daughter to sleep in their bed at night, saying that it would stifle her recuperation. "Only in the most dire of circumstances," is what she told them.

Dan and Susan Rodgers knew that this was certainly one of those circumstances.

Shortly after her mom began reading aloud her favorite *Curious George* book, Briana fell back to sleep. Mr. Teddy, as always, lay nestled beside her.

A little while later, Dan Rodgers lifted his head from his pillow and whispered to his wife, "I'm going to sleep in Briana's room."

Then he pointed to the glaring overhead light, which they had promised Briana would stay on all night, to make known his reason.

Susan Rodgers nodded her head and mouthed a silent "I love you."

Then she cuddled up next to her daughter and fell fast asleep.

CHAPTER 80

As the time neared eleven p.m., his patience neared its limit.

He knew that the others, though still silent, couldn't hold out much longer, either.

"What the fuck are they doing up there?" he muttered.

Then he picked up a handful of soil and squeezed it in his clenched hand. Slowly, he let the dirt trickle down between his fingers.

He picked up another handful and repeated the process.

Then he came up with an idea!

The soil would serve as the sand, and his soil-filled hands, the hourglass. As slowly as possible, he would let the sand pass through the hourglass. If the bedroom light was not turned off by the time that all the sand had trickled through the hourglass, then the act would be postponed.

He assured the others that if such a postponement were necessary, then his next attempt would be even more daring than this one was to be.

CHAPTER 81

Most of the tears that Dan Rodgers shed were shed in solitude. Tonight was no exception. Briana's hellish nightmare had saddened him so, her suffering made his own feel that much more pronounced.

As he lay in his daughter's bed, with his eyes reddened from the dried-up tears, he thought back to that morning. He had left the house at his usual time, drove the usual twenty minutes to his office, sipped his coffee as he glanced through his newspaper, and then started his workday. Just like he did every day.

Then came the phone call.

The only thing that brought him any refuge at all was the thought that, one day, the killer would be caught.

Unable to fall asleep in the room that his daughter once shared with her beloved twin sister, he threw on his bathrobe and walked down the long steep staircase to the living room.

He stood in front of the liquor cabinet and studied its contents.

Then he reached up and grabbed a bottle of Johnnie Walker Black from the top shelf.

He opened the bottle and chugged down as much as he could.

Then he chugged down some more. And some more after that.

Unable to stand on his own accord, he stumbled over to the wall and leaned up against it. Using the wall as his guide, he made his way to the staircase.

One little step at a time, he staggered up the stairs.

When he got to the top, he leaned his back against the hallway wall and stumbled his way into his bedroom.

Then he flicked off the light and plopped down on the bed, beside his wife and daughter.

CHAPTER 82

The bedroom window turned to darkness.

Quickly, he released the soil from his hand and rubbed his hands together to clean off the dirt. Using only his front teeth, he pulled the thin black glove a tad tighter, and then removed the ski mask from his front pocket and tugged it over his head.

When it was positioned correctly, with his eyes able to see through the small round holes, he couldn't resist the urge to stick his tongue out through the small slit provided. The others couldn't control themselves. They laughed hysterically at the image of the faceless tongue.

In a manner reminiscent of a magician, he displayed a long roll of thin string. He wrapped it around the glove on his left hand, and then held it up for the others to see.

Loudly, they cheered.

Then, keeping as close to the ground as possible, he ventured towards the house. His eyes focused on the small, rectangular basement window.

Upon arriving at his destination, he lay down on his side.

With his weight resting on his left elbow, he lifted up his right foot and pressed it down on the pane of the small casement window. He was careful not to exert too much pressure, so as to not cause it to fling open too quickly and make too much noise.

When he felt the window push open a crack, he leaned over and reached his hand inside. With his glove-covered fingers, he felt around for the latch that kept it from opening more fully. He grinned as his fingers unlocked the latch - a much easier task than expected. His grin widened when he peeked down at the washing machine, sitting just below the window.

He slid through the open window and planted his feet on top of the machine. Then he squatted down upon it, and looked ahead into the partial darkness.

A long staircase sat in the center of the large, unfinished basement.

Slowly, he slid off the washing machine and crept towards the staircase, and then up the steep stairs.

When he got to the top, he inched open the door and stuck

his head out.   Seeing that all appeared safe, he ventured into the dark hallway.

On the tips of his toes, he made his way to the staircase that led up to the bedrooms.

He looked up the stairs but saw nothing, just darkness.

Like a cat venturing into the unknown, he made his ascent, one step at a time.   When he reached the top, he felt his way through the dark hallway until he came upon Briana's bedroom.

The door had been left open.   A small night-light in the corner of the room shed just enough light for him to see.

Slowly, he crept towards her bed.

"Where the hell is she?" he sneered as he sat, crouched, next to the empty bed.

When the shock wore off, he tiptoed to the other side of the bed, away from the doorway. There he sat, with his back against the wall.

"She must be sleeping in mommy and daddy's room."

"Now, what do we do?" the voice asked.

"Shut up! That's what you'll do.   You'll shut your mouth and let me handle this."

"As you wish, sissy boy."

He took a few deep breaths to calm himself down. He knew that he needed to remain calm in order to keep the others at bay.

He pondered going through with the act, despite it all. The prospect of doing so exhilarated him, yet its risk caused him much anxiety. Back and forth, the question of what to do ping-ponged in his mind.

"How about a little eeny-meeny-miney-moe, sissy boy?"

He forced himself to ignore the comment, knowing that continuing to do otherwise would only serve to fuel their cause. He knew as well that he must soon reach a decision in order to quell their wrath.

Alas, he made up his mind. Since all of the sand did not flow through the hourglass, the act would be postponed.

Proud of himself for reaching a decision, he crept towards the open doorway.   When he got to the hallway, he tiptoed ahead, using the wall to guide him through the darkness.

When he reached the staircase, he extended his arm to

grab hold of the wooden railing. But his left hand, bound in string and a thin black glove, failed to grab it, causing him to lose his balance.

He fell forward, unable to regain his balance, and tumbled headfirst down the steep flight of stairs!

Frantically, upon reaching the bottom, he shot up and darted toward the rear door.

It wouldn't open. The top deadbolt needed a key to unlock it from the inside. So he hurried down the basement stairs, jumped onto the washing machine and then pulled himself up and through the open window.

Once outside, he stumbled and then ran like the wind towards the high, white picket fence. He leaped over it, quite effortlessly, as if it were but a fraction of its size.

Hurrying to the street, he began his full-speed journey.

As the sweat poured down his forehead and trickled into his eyes, he made his way to the rear of the strip mall. He stood there, hidden behind a large trash container, and wiped the perspiration from his face.

Then he walked through the parking lot to his car.

The voices kept silent for the duration of his drive home.

As soon as he arrived there, however, they made up for lost time.

"Better get out the string, daddy, it's time for fun and games."

He took off his black shirt and white collar, and let them fall to the floor beside the bed.

Weeping like a little child, he lay there, faceup and motionless his arms outstretched.

He grimaced when he felt the force tie the string around his genitals.

Slowly, the force tightened the string, tighter and tighter and tighter.

"Please take it off! I beg of you!" he screamed.

"You deserve no pity. You stupid, clumsy fool."

"Next time, the twin will die, like her sister! I promise!"

"Sure she will, sissy boy."

"While mommy and daddy are watching!"

167

The string began to loosen, the magic words having been spoken.

CHAPTER 83

"Sergeant Miller, there's been a break-in at the Rodgers' residence."

A bucketful of ice water poured on my bare body couldn't have gotten me out of bed any faster.

Penny shot up when I turned on the light.

"What's going on?" she asked, her hands cupped over her eyes to block out the light.

"Someone broke into the home of one of the victims."

"Oh my God! Which one?"

"Briane Rodgers."

"Oh my God!" she yelled as she popped her naked body out of bed and began throwing her clothes on.

"What are you doing?" I asked.

"I'm coming with you, Max. Okay?"

She was already halfway dressed by the time that I got a chance to respond, her way of telling me that "no" was not going to be a viable answer.

"What for?" I asked, despite myself.

"If there's been a break-in at the home of a family whose daughter, a twin sister, was found hanged to death, then I think it would be fair to assume that a mental health professional might serve some useful purpose there."

"Yeah, I guess," I replied.

Then I stood up and grabbed my keys off of the dresser.

"Ready?" I asked as she stood in front of the closet door mirror, brushing her hair.

"Two seconds," she replied.

She walked over to me, grabbed hold of my shoulder and slipped her shoes on. As soon as she let go, I turned and hurried down the hallway, and then out front door.

Penny was with me every step of the way.

CHAPTER 84

By the time that we arrived there, the street was already smothered with police and emergency vehicles. Their flashing overhead lights illuminated the sky like it was the Fourth of July. I parked my Vette a few houses down from the Rodgers' residence, which was as close as I could get.

As Penny and I did a fast walk towards the Rodgers' home, I heard someone shout, "Detective Miller!"

I spotted him right away. It was Officer Gorman, the plainclothes cop who had stopped to question me on the night that I sat in my car in front of the Rodgers' home.

We walked over to the sidewalk where he was standing.

"What the hell happened?" I shouted.

His face reddened so that I thought for sure that the young officer was going down for the count. But he managed to regain his composure rather quickly.

"He got in through the basement window, in the rear of the house. I was patrolling the front."

"So, you didn't see or hear anything?"

"Nothing, Detective."

"Jesus Christ! What were you doing while all of this was going on, playing with yourself?"

Penny grabbed hold of my arm. The tighter that she gripped it, the more thought I gave to the words that were about to flow from my lips. She was right - telling off the young officer was accomplishing absolutely nothing. So I said,

"By the way, Officer Gorman, it's now Sergeant Miller."

With a look of relief on his face, he extended his hand to me.

"Congratulations, Sergeant."

"Thanks."

Then we parted company.

When we came upon the Rodgers' home, I stepped over the police tape that sealed off the front lawn and then turned around to help Penny over it. There were a half a dozen or so uniformed officers holding flashlights, looking around the premises. I held up my badge as we walked to the front door, for the sake of anyone who didn't know who I was.

As soon as we walked through the front door, I caught sight

170

of Noodle. He's a tough sight to miss. He and Saladino were standing in the living room. The Rodgers were seated on the sofa across from them.

As we approached, I could see Briana sitting there with her face buried in her mother's lap. Briana's dad, who was seated on the other side of his wife, could barely keep his eyes open. His body started to tilt forward, but he snapped back up as he caught himself beginning to doze.

Saladino and Noodle turned to face us.

"The guy got in through the basement window, in the rear of the house. The kid was asleep in her parents' room when it happened," Saladino said.

"Thank God for that," Penny replied.

My reply was not as serene.

"How the fuck could someone possibly break in?"

Penny once again grabbed hold of my arm, to shut me up.

After she let go, she walked over to Mrs. Rodgers and introduced herself.

Then she knelt down in front of Briana.

In a soft, consoling voice, she said, "What a nice teddy bear. What's its name?"

Briana lifted her head, slightly.

"Mr. Teddy," she whispered.

A smile broke out on her pretty little face.

Mrs. Rodgers stroked her daughter's long, curly blonde hair as Penny consoled her. The poor kid needed all the comforting that she could get.

Claude, who I had called from my car phone on the way there, walked through the front door. I walked over to him and motioned for him to follow me outside. Then I turned to Noodle and Saladino, and motioned for them to do the same.

When we got outside, I instructed the three of them to start knocking on the neighbors' doors to find out if any of them saw or heard anything. Out of the corner of my eye, I spotted a news camera coming towards the house. So I hurried back inside.

I looked over at Penny. She was still consoling the poor kid. So I headed down, to the basement.

I couldn't believe my eyes when I caught sight of the

171

washing machine sitting there below the window. They might as well have put a welcome mat on the top of it.

After looking around the basement for a little while, I walked back up the stairs and made my way into the backyard.

As I looked around the yard, I came to a *definite* conclusion - Father Stanton wasn't our guy.

Although this seemed to be more and more obvious as time went on, it wasn't until that night that I ruled him out completely. No one in Father Stanton's frail condition could have hopped over the white picket fence that surrounded the yard. It looked to be five feet high. It couldn't have been someone with a sizable weight problem, either. Aside from not making it over the fence, there's no way that he would have fit through the small basement window.

It had to be someone in fairly decent shape.

As I walked towards the front of the house to feed some news to the media people, I thought about my conversation with Claude. My prediction that the guy was going to become more daring, in order to fulfill his mind's demented appetite, had become a reality. With this attempt having gone awry, there was not a trace of doubt in my mind or my gut that his rage, now fueled by his failed attempt, would be the foundation upon which his next act would be built.

CHAPTER 85

Penny began spending a good deal of her free time trying to locate Jill, primarily via the Internet. As a law enforcement officer, I knew firsthand that she had her work cut out for her. Searching for a woman of Jill's age can be especially tough because her last name might have changed due to marriage. Having had no idea as to which part of the country (or the world, for that matter) she now inhabited didn't exactly do much to help our cause. Penny, however, insisted that the odds were good that Jill lived somewhere in the state of New York. She told me that most young adults still tend to settle in, or near, the area that they were raised. Since Jill grew up on Long Island and in Buffalo, Penny surmised that she was probably living somewhere in New York State.

As far as the break-in at the Rodgers' residence was concerned, I took the liberty of turning the place into a fortress to make certain that it didn't happen again. I assigned eighteen officers in total to patrol the house six at a time, in eight-hour shifts. To be doubly sure that the backyard would not again be used to gain access to the house, I not only had the basement window bolted, but I also had one officer stationed in front of it around the clock. He was instructed not to let himself wander off the patio, except in the case of a dire emergency.

If someone were looking for a place to gain unauthorized entry, they'd have been better off giving Fort Knox a try.

The Rodgers had no problem whatsoever with the added security. They welcomed it, in fact. They did make one request, however, that they be allowed to attend church services on Sunday mornings without police presence. This was their time to be alone with their memories of Briane.

Otherwise, all was pretty much status quo for the week or two that followed the break-in.

This was something that I found no solace in whatsoever. To the contrary, status quo, to me, meant one thing and one thing only - he was in the planning stage of what his sick and twisted mind surely viewed as his next act of heroism. It left me with a most uneasy feeling, like I was sitting right smack in the eye of a hurricane, where all was quiet but not calm. The storm was taking a short reprieve, conserving its energy in order to strengthen its wrath.

CHAPTER 86

The fact that I once caught a foul ball at Yankee Stadium does not, in itself, lend a great deal of relevance to the topic at hand.

The feeling that I experienced upon catching that foul ball is where such relevance neatly comes into play. I was overcome by that very same feeling the very moment that I caught sight of Tara Shiver's dad and brother, Derek, walking into my office on that rainy Monday morning.

As soon as that foul ball was hit, I knew that it was headed right at me. But up until the very moment that it landed squarely in my hands, I was unsure as to whether or not it would meet such a fate. In that same light, I was all but certain that Derek Shiver had something on his mind that he wanted to divulge to me. But up until that glorious moment that he and his dad stepped into my office, I couldn't say for sure if such a moment would ever come into being.

Although my feeling of elation was certainly more intense in this instance, it was, of course, displayed in a much more restrained manner. As much as I would have liked to pick up little Derek and proudly show him off for all to see, such was not a real viable option. That is not to say, however, that I made any attempt whatsoever to suppress the ear-to-ear smile that surfaced on my face as I stood up to greet him.

"How's my fellow Yankee fan doing?" I asked as I shook his tiny hand.

"Good," he replied.

I reached over to shake his dad's hand. Then I asked the two of them to have a seat.

Mr. Shiver came right out and spoke the very same words that he had spoken the day after the murder of his one and only daughter.

"Derek has something that he'd like to tell you."

Unlike the last time, however, Derek didn't give a shy glance to his dad for the go-ahead to start speaking. Rather, in a loud, confident voice, he said, "The guy looked at me."

Such were the most beautiful words that I'd ever heard spoken. It was as if Mozart and Beethoven had just synergized into one.

Then, just like I did when Lisa Sanchez sat in that very same chair and spoke her shocking words, I cleared my throat to remove the nervous tickle that was stuck there before I spoke.

"Do you remember what he looks like, Derek?"

"Yeah. I think I do."

"Okay then, how about if you, me and your dad walk upstairs and meet with an artist, so that she can draw a picture of him."

"Okay," he replied.

I looked over at Glen Shiver for his okay. With a smile on his face, he gave his nod of approval. I could not have imagined how much the guy's capture would mean to him. But, I knew that the very thought of it happening was enough to bring a smile to the face of this badly beaten man.

I wanted very much to ask how his wife was doing but held back the question for a more appropriate time, when young Derek didn't have to be subjected to such conversation.

"Where's the Mets guy?" Derek asked.

I smiled and said, "He's right down the hallway. Want to stop by his office and see if he wants to go upstairs with us?"

"Okay," Derek quickly replied.

"Shall we?" I asked.

Then I stood up to lead the way.

CHAPTER 87

Katie Avero was not only a gifted artist, but a top-notch photographer as well. Being that she was a full-time employee of the Nassau County Police Department, an overwhelming majority of her time was spent shooting and developing photographs of crime scenes, her artistic talent only being needed in rare instances such as this one.

Although Katie's daily attire, denim jeans and a white lab coat, was easy to predict, the same could not be said about her hair color. She seemed to change it about as often as most people change their socks and underwear.

"What have we here, a redhead?" I asked, in the most unserious of tones, as we stepped into her office.

"Better watch out. You know what they say about us redheads," Katie playfully replied.

Then Claude made a triumphant attempt at loosening up little Derek by putting on his most effeminate-sounding voice and saying, "My goodness, what a coincidence! I, too, was toying with the idea of becoming a redhead; think it's for me, little fella?"

Derek had himself one heck of a good, old-fashioned belly laugh. It was as uplifting a sight as I'd witnessed in quite some time. When he was eventually all laughed out, I introduced the young lad and his father to Katie.

"Derek has a picture that he'd like you to draw, Katie," I said.

Katie stood up from her desk and walked over to Derek. Then she knelt down in front of him and looked into his eyes.

"Ready to help me draw my picture, Derek?"

"Yup," he replied.

Hand in hand, they walked over to the corner of the room, towards Katie's easel. I had spoken with Katie about Derek soon after Tara's funeral, so she knew exactly why he was there and what her job was to be.

"Derek, where were you when you saw the man?" Katie asked as she stood in front of her canvas, with the young lad by her side.

"In my backyard."

"Now, if you make believe that this is your backyard and this is your house," she said as she drew on the canvas, "I'd like you to show me where the man was standing when you saw his face."

"Ummm, over there," Derek replied, as he pointed to a spot on the canvas.

"And where were you standing, Derek?"

"Over here."

"All right, Derek, now I'd like for you to sit down and close your eyes. Try to imagine that you're standing in your backyard. Make believe that you're standing at the very same spot that you showed me."

After he was seated, with his eyes closed, Katie allowed him ample time to concentrate. Then she asked, "Are you standing there, Derek?"

"Yup."

"Now try to picture the man standing in the very same spot that you saw him."

In due time, she asked, "Are you able to do that, Derek?"

"Yeah, I think so."

"What can you tell me about the color of his hair?"

"Ummm, it's black, like my friend Brian's."

For a good ten minutes, Derek sat there, answering Katie's questions as she sketched his descriptions onto the canvas. Then she asked him to stand up and take a look at the portrait.

With Derek serving as her guide, Katie spent quite some time touching it up. When all the finishing touches had at last been made, Katie looked over at me and said, "Here's what we've got, Max."

As I stood there, looking the portrait of the coward in the eye, I wanted to reach forward and rip him to pieces and then squeeze his crumpled remains in my hand.

I couldn't even begin to fathom what was going through the mind of Tara's dad, who was standing there beside me.

CHAPTER 88

I wasn't given the opportunity to sit down and really scrutinize the portrait until late that afternoon. Up until then, the public relations guys needed access to it, in order to circulate copies of it to the media.

Being that Katie drew the portrait via a secondhand description, it didn't have that photo-like quality which paintings of still subjects often do. Nonetheless, there was something about it that kept drawing me back to it. I would put it aside, only to pick it back up a minute or two later.

His dark, beady eyes, I soon came to realize, were the cause of my obsessive behavior. Katie's portrait was not the first place that I had seen them. They belonged to someone that I knew or someone that I had, at least, looked at long enough for such a feature to make an imprint on my mind.

So I buzzed Claude on the intercom and told him to come to my office.

"Nothing about him rings a bell, Max," he said after studying the drawing. Being that Claude and I had been partners for eleven years, I had high hopes for a totally different response. I was anticipating something like, "Yeah, he looks like someone we once booked," or at the very least, "I know what you mean about him looking familiar."

"You sure?" I asked, encouraging him to take another look.

I studied Claude's face as he looked it over again.

"You know something? On second thought, maybe there is something about him that looks familiar."

"His eyes, perhaps?"

"Yeah, his eyes...and his eyebrows."

"Yeah, you're right! Those heavy eyebrows as well."

After Claude placed the portrait back down on my desk, I said, "Penny's been trying to locate Jill for me."

I knew Claude well enough to know that his silence didn't mean that he had nothing to say on the matter, but rather whether or not he should say it.

Finally, he spoke.

"You think it's a real good time for her to be doing that?"

"I didn't at first, but Penny convinced me otherwise. I trust her opinion very much."

"I don't blame you, she's one of the best."

"She's the best, my friend."

"I guess the Sarge knew what he was talking about."

It took me a few seconds to figure out what he meant.

"You know something? For some reason, I hadn't given a moment's thought to what the Sarge had said about Penny and me."

"Well, I sure hadn't forgotten how shocked you were when he told you that he thought that Penny was the right woman for you."

"Did you ever meet a smarter guy than Earl?" I asked.

"Never."

"Me neither. Man, do I miss him."

"You and me both, Max."

"The killings began too damn close in time to Betsy's death. He was still in the mourning stage. As you well know, the Sarge's suicide did one good job in screwing up my mind. It was the very last thing I needed during this fucking nightmare of a case. That's why Penny thought that now would be a good time for us to try and locate Jill."

"Yeah, it'll give you something else to think about."

"It actually goes a lot deeper than that, Claude. The Sarge was still mourning the death of his wife when all this began. That much I knew. What I didn't know, however, was that I, too, have been in mourning. Unlike the Sarge, though, I've been mourning someone who's still alive, someone who I love and cherish every bit as much as Glen Shiver and Dan Rodgers loved and cherished their little girls."

CHAPTER 89

We were counting on the media to give as many people as was humanly possible the opportunity to get a look at Katie's drawing.

That they did.

Every local newspaper in the area displayed it on the front page. That was in addition to all the local television stations airing it on their evening news telecasts. CNN, Fox, MSNBC and all of the other national news stations also chose to show their viewers the picture of the man who had become known throughout the country as "The Long Island Hangman."

Our 800 tip line phone number, which we had asked the media to display alongside his picture, was ringing at a steady pace throughout the day. A good number of those calls, I was told, came from women who claimed that the guy looked like their ex-husbands. No surprise there.

At about 4:30 that afternoon, one of the callers asked to speak with me personally.

When I heard the voice on the other end of the line, it felt like "déjà vu all over again." It was Sister Rosemary.

"I just saw the picture in the newspaper. I need to speak with you about it."

"Sure, go right ahead."

"I'd feel more comfortable talking to you in person."

Staying calm was becoming a difficult task in itself, so I put my hand over the mouthpiece of the phone and cleared my throat, "Would you like me to come to you, Sister Rosemary? I can be there within the hour."

"No, not here. Someplace else."

"Just tell me where, and I'll be there."

"Well, I don't drive so...."

"Sister Rosemary, are you familiar with the coffee shop that's located a block or two south of the school? I believe it's called Margo's."

"Yes, it's right next to the laundromat on 73rd Avenue."

"That's the one. Can you meet me there?"

"I'm not sure how late they're open."

"If the coffee shop is closed, then meet me at the

laundromat next door. I'm sure that it stays open late."

"What time shall we meet?"

"Anytime you want."

My words were followed by a dead silence.

"Hello," I said to make sure that she was still on the line.

"Yes, I'm still here. Let me see. Can we make it tomorrow, perhaps?"

I thought for a moment.

"No. Let's make it sometime tonight, please."

I didn't want to give her all that time to reconsider.

"It'll have to be after the girls go to bed."

"What time is that?"

"Nine o'clock."

"I'll meet you at nine-thirty. Okay?"

She didn't respond.

"Nine-thirty, okay?"

"Nine-thirty it is."

CHAPTER 90

The wrought iron gate which sealed off the front of the coffee shop provided about as blatant an indication that business hours were over as I was likely to find. Luckily though, the brightly lit sign on the window of the laundromat read "Open 24 hours, 7 days a week."

Noticing that there were a few people inside the laundromat, I chose to remain in my unmarked police car to await Sister Rosemary's arrival. It wasn't until almost ten o'clock that I caught sight of her walking towards the entrance of the laundromat. Being that I was starting to get some serious doubts as to whether or not she was going to show, I was more than just a little happy to see her. So I rolled down the passenger side window and shouted out her name.

As she turned to look, I flicked on the inside light so that she could see me. As she approached, I pulled open the door handle and pushed open the door for her. After she sat herself down in the passenger seat, she made an unsuccessful attempt at closing the heavy door, so I hopped out and trotted around to the passenger side to slam it shut.

"I apologize for my tardiness. Something's always coming up that requires my attention," she said when I sat back down in the driver's seat.

"No need to apologize. I passed by a little diner on the way here. It's about a mile or two south on the corner of Northern Boulevard. It looks like a good place for us to talk in private."

"Oh yes, I know the place. That sounds fine with me."

So without further delay, I pulled away from the curb and headed due south.

CHAPTER 91

There was barely a soul in the diner when we got there. But I still felt it wise for us to sit in the very last booth, away from the entrance. I closed the blinds after we sat down, in order to block out any view of us from the outside.

The waitress came over right away. Sister Rosemary ordered a cup of hot tea. Since this was no time to be stuffing my face, I had to make do with just a cup of coffee.

As the waitress walked back to the counter, Sister Rosemary began her tale without any coaxing from me.

"I believe that I know the person on the front page of The Daily News."

Containing my excitement was no easy task. But I knew how important it was for me to appear calm. A calmer investigator meant a calmer subject.

"Do you know his name?"

"Unfortunately not."

"Please go on," I said.

"Up until about twelve years ago, I was with the Saint James Church, on the West Side of Manhattan. The parish ran a home for troubled teenagers, most of them runaways. I believe that one of the youths who lived in the home was the person shown in the newspaper. Naturally he was quite a bit younger back then, but his face hasn't changed all that much."

"How many kids lived in the home?"

"Usually about forty or so at one time. But different kids were coming and going all the time. So over the course of a year, there were a couple of hundred, at least."

Sister Rosemary looked down for a moment. Then she lifted her head back up and looked deep into my eyes, as if she were searching for the soul within.

"Terrible things took place in the home."

As soon as she got the last syllable out, she broke down. Being that I was not in a very consoling mood, I just sat there, waiting for her to continue.

"Many of the boys were sexually abused by a couple of the parish's priests. Nothing was done about it. Except, that is, to transfer these priests to different parishes. The sinners were forgiven, just like that, but at whose expense? Young boys?"

"Perhaps a lot more than that," I thought.

"He told us to keep silent for the sake of the Church and the Lord. How hypocritical of him! How despicable!"

"Who? Who told you to keep silent?"

"The head priest of the church."

"What was his name?"

"Father Peter Rhiner. He passed away a number of years ago."

Sister Rosemary was fuming with anger, much to my delight. Anger is often an investigator's closest ally because it's often accompanied by candidness.

"It was a sin every bit as sinful as the act committed by the abusers themselves. To think that the person responsible for the vicious killings of those innocent little girls may be one of the boys that had been abused at Saint James makes me furious, more furious than I've ever been in my entire life."

She paused for a few seconds, then looked back up at me and said, "There's something else that I think you'd be interested in knowing."

Rather than responding, I let the silence run its course.

"Claudia's mother, Lisa Sanchez lived there as well."

That nervous tickle immediately found its way into my esophagus when she said that. So I cleared my throat and asked, "At the same time?"

"Yes, I believe so. She was there much longer than he was, though. I don't believe that he was there for too long a period of time."

I wonder why, I thought to myself.

"Lisa was the only person from Saint James that I maintained any contact with."

"How often did you speak with her?"

"Initially, once a month or so. But over time, we spoke less and less frequently."

"When did she tell you about Claudia?"

"She called me a few months after she had given birth, which happened to be about the same time that I had become affiliated with the school. After that, I would make mention of the school whenever we'd speak. I figured that if her daughter

185

was as bright as she was, then she'd be an ideal candidate."

"Did she tell you who Claudia's father was?"

"No, I had once asked her and her response seemed like a polite way of telling me to mind my own business."

"Do you remember what she said?"

"She said that it was a man that she'd known for many years. That was it. Then she quickly changed the subject."

I knew my next question was a shot in the dark, but I asked it anyway.

"Have you ever given confession to Father Ken Vecchia?"

"No, never. I've never even heard the name before."

"Is the group home still there?"

"No, it was closed years ago, just after I left."

"How about the church?"

"I assume that it's still there, but everyone who was affiliated with it back then is long gone. They wanted no skeletons in their closets."

"Can you think of anyone other than Lisa Sanchez who might recall his name?"

She shook her head.

"How about the abusers themselves?" I asked.

"As sad as it sounds, I don't know their real names. After they were transferred out, I learned that their names had been changed before they joined our parish. They changed them once again after they were transferred out of Saint James. From the looks of things, it seems that the only person that I can think of who would know his name is Lisa Sanchez."

CHAPTER 92

I dropped Sister Rosemary off by the main entrance of the school. As soon as she walked through the front door, I called Penny from my cell phone.

"How'd it go?" she asked.

"I think I need your help to sort things out."

"Where are you now?"

"Jackson Heights. I just dropped her off a minute ago."

"I'll meet you at your place."

I arrived at my home a little before Penny did. After I opened the door to let her in, we stood in the small foyer hugging each other, about as tightly as we could have without causing serious injury to one another. It was the longest that we'd gone without seeing each other since we became an item, a whole three days.

"What do you say we stay like this forever?" she whispered.

"Sister Rosemary knows who the guy is," I whispered back.

She quickly released me from her grasp.

"Oh my God, Max! Oh my God!"

"He looks like someone that she knew a number of years ago. Let's sit down," I said.

I held her hand and led the way to the living room couch.

As soon as we were seated, Penny asked, "Does she know his name?"

"No such luck. The guy lived in a group home for teenage runaways which was run by a church in Manhattan that she was with at the time. A young lady whose name you've heard before lived there at the same time. Want to take a stab at it, doc?"

"Initials L.S.?"

"Bingo!"

"Is there anyone else that she knows of who might remember his name?"

"Nope."

"Is the home still around?"

"Nope. It seems that there were certain goings-on there that took place behind closed doors."

"Oh no, don't tell me!"

"I have to. It would be rather hypocritical of me to keep it a secret. A couple of the priests were molesting the boys that lived there."

"Is there anything sicker than that?" the renowned Roman Catholic psychiatrist asked.

"Yeah."

"What?"

"Shoving the molesters off to other parishes, and then standing in front of the pulpit on Sunday mornings to preach to others how they should live their lives."

After a brief silence, Penny said, "Are you ready for my suggestion of what to do next?"

"I sure am."

"We go on television and plead for someone to come forward who can help solve the case. We tell the people exactly what we now know, namely that the guy had been molested by a couple of priests in a group home when he was younger. We also tell them that a young lady named Lisa Sanchez, who's missing, lived in that very same home."

"What exactly is that going to accomplish?"

"It might very well cause someone, such as that woman at confession, to come forward."

"How do you figure?"

"The fact that there's now a definite, identifiable connection between Lisa and the killer might very well cause this woman to see things in a totally different light."

"I just thought of something! If Lisa knew who he was all along, then why the hell didn't she just tell me, instead of making up some bullshit story about some bullshit dreams that she was having?"

"With all the havoc that this guy must have created in her life, I think that there's a real good chance that her mental condition wasn't very stable. You can just imagine how petrified she must have been. God only knows what was going on in the mind of a person in her condition. So we mustn't draw any conclusions about her motives until we know the whole story."

"Yeah, I get what you're saying. If this mystery woman does

know more than she's letting on, do you really think that we can get her to finally let it out?"

"I certainly hope so, Max."

CHAPTER 93

The bright lights of the news cameras were a lot easier to contend with this time around. The fact that I was good and ready for them certainly had a lot to do with it. After I said a few words, I gave Penny her plug.

"I'd now like to introduce you to Dr. Penny Forrester. Dr. Forrester is a professor of psychiatry at the State University of New York at Stony Brook. She is working closely with us in trying to put an end to these horrific murders."

Penny squeezed my arm as she walked by me to get to the microphones; probably to calm herself down, this time.

"Good evening. What I'm about to say is meant for one person in particular. This person has twice given confession to a local priest, the contents of which Sergeant Miller and I are fully aware. Some might feel that this priest has committed a sin by coming forward and revealing this confidential information to us. If you think it's a sin to try and save little girls from being hanged to death, then I guess you're correct.

"As we are all well aware, certain men of the clergy used their religion as a vehicle by which to gain sexual gratification at the expense of little boys and young men. We are also aware of the fact that certain men of the clergy who knew of this despicable behavior chose to do nothing about it. Worse yet, some who knew chose to transfer these pedophiles to other parishes where they'd be free to repeat their sexual misconduct.

"Based on extremely reliable information that we've received, we strongly believe that the man responsible for these horrific murders was himself abused by members of the clergy. This abuse, of which we just recently learned, took place during his adolescence, while he was living in a group home. A young lady by the name of Lisa Sanchez was living there as well. Ms. Sanchez is the only person that we know of who can positively identify the killer.

"In closing, I'd like to tell that someone who's been holding back information from us to please keep in mind that your silence is allowing these brutal murders to continue."

CHAPTER 94

He lay in bed, staring at the small television in front of him. It baffled him to no end how the woman on the screen knew of the abuse that had been forced upon him. He wondered if this woman was somehow able to hear his thoughts.

"That's crazy. You're not crazy. Are you?" the voice shouted.

"Shut up!" he screamed back.

The voice would not listen.

"Maybe Lisa or Claudia told her. Maybe the doctor woman can communicate with the dead."

The giggles of the others flooded his brain.

"Who says they're dead, you babbling fools?"

Their giggles turned to hysterics.

Unwilling to put up with their torture any longer, he shot out of bed and ran to the dresser. Quickly, he threw on the black shirt and white collar. Then he walked back to his bed, clicked off the television and laid back down.

As he lay there, with his head resting in his cupped hands, he saw neither the badly peeled paint nor the slight flickering of the fluorescent light on the ceiling above him. All that he could visualize was the small, dark bedroom of Briana Rodgers.

Getting the twin had become his unyielding obsession ever since the night of that failed attempt. The fact that the police now knew of his desire to get Briana made the task that much more challenging.

He loved the challenge. It filled him with a renewed sense of passion and lust.

He knew that the others cherished it as much as he.

CHAPTER 95

She sat in her parked car, next to the rear entrance of the church. The windshield wipers, flopping back and forth at full speed, served little purpose. They were no match for the heavy, windswept rain.

The car's engine was still running. She was not sure if she would be able to get herself to turn it off. The reason had nothing to do with the outside conditions. It was something deep within that was immobilizing her. Something that came about long before the unborn child began developing inside of her.

She looked over at the clock on the dashboard. It read 9:43. At 10:00, she would either drive away or shut off the engine and enter the church, to carry out her intentions.

CHAPTER 96

The rain washed away any hopes of Claude and me getting in nine holes of golf, as we had planned. Penny had already informed me that she was going to be spending the day with her daughter, so it seemed like the perfect opportunity to relax in my easy chair and watch some football. So I threw on a pair of shorts and a raincoat and headed over to the nearby 7-Eleven to pick up some of life's finer things, like beer and chips and donuts.

When I returned home, I noticed that the message indicator was flashing on my answering machine. Being that I was all set to enjoy a day of doing nothing, it took some effort on my part to get myself to press my finger down on that little button.

"Max, it's Ken Vecchia. Call me at the church when you get this message."

Unlike the last message that he left, Ken's voice sounded rather calm and tranquil. Almost too tranquil. So I dialed his number without delay.

"I need to speak with you, Max. Can you come over to the church?"

"Absolutely, Ken. I can be there in less than an hour. What's up?"

"We'll talk when you get here."

"You okay?"

"Yes, I'm fine. Come in through the back entrance."

"I'm leaving right now, Ken."

CHAPTER 97

I entered the church through the rear entrance, as Ken had requested. When he heard me call out his name, he stepped out into the hallway.

We shook hands. Then he said, "The woman came back, Max."

"When?"

"This morning. She said that she'd like to speak with you."

"Did she leave her address or phone number?"

"She's still here, Max."

"Where?"

"Follow me."

Ken led me to the room where the clergyman customarily sits during confessions.

"Have a seat, Max. She's in the booth, waiting for you."

After I sat down in the chair, beside the screen, Ken turned around and walked out of the room, closing the door behind him. It felt awfully strange to be sitting on the receiving side of a confessional.

"My name's Sergeant Max Miller. I'm with the Nassau County Police Department. Father Vecchia told me that you'd like to speak with me."

"I know Lisa Sanchez," the disguised voice replied.

"What's your name?"

"That's not important."

"How do you know Lisa?"

"I work with her at North Shore Hospital."

"You've been here before, haven't you?"

"Yes."

"Why won't you reveal your identity?"

A dead silence set in before she responded.

"I have my reasons. They have nothing to do with the matter at hand, though."

"Do you know of any men in Lisa's life?"

"None that I can recall her mentioning. I do know that she has a daughter, though."

"She told you so?"

"Yes. She'd told me about Claudia."

"Did she mention anything to you about the school that Claudia attended?"

"Yes. She told me that it was affiliated with the Church and that Claudia lived there."

"Had Lisa ever spoken to you about any of the dreams that she'd been having?"

"Yes, she did. She told me about a priest that she'd been seeing in her dreams. I had a feeling that she knew more than she was letting on, though."

"What made you feel that way?"

"Nothing in particular. A gut feeling, so to speak."

Ironically enough, it was that very same feeling that led to my next question.

"Did you advise Lisa to tell me about the dreams that she'd been talking to you about?"

"Yes, I did."

It was time to put her to the test, to see if she was for real.

"Have you ever been to Lisa's apartment?"

"Just once."

"How long ago?"

"Last winter."

"Can you describe it to me?"

"Small, one bedroom, tiny kitchenette."

"How many beds were in her bedroom?"

"I couldn't say. The bedroom door was closed at the time."

"Did you get to see...."

"The bedroom door was broken, come to think of it."

"Broken in what way?"

"The bottom was smashed in. It looked like it was kicked in, actually."

Her words struck me with the power of a full-force tornado, causing my mind to race back in time. I envisioned the damaged door as it looked on the day of Lisa's disappearance. It wasn't like that the first time that I was there.

"You still there?"

"Yeah, I'm sorry. The door - did you happen to ask Lisa how it got in that condition? How it got banged in like that?"

"No. I didn't feel like prying. I wish I had, though. I wish I had pried like hell, about a lot of things."

"Don't we all. So how can I get in touch with you?"

"I'll get in touch with you."

I agreed to allow her to leave the building while I remained in the booth. I cheated a little though, by peeking through the screen as she turned to open the door.

The black veil may have hidden her face, but there was no disguising the fact that she was going to be bringing a child into the world in the very near future.

CHAPTER 98

I wasn't exactly doing the speed limit on my ride back home, or anything close to it. Despite how fast my Vette was traveling, my mind was moving at a much faster speed.

Trying to figure out who the woman was whom I'd just spoken with was driving me up a wall. The fact that she did one hell of a good job disguising her voice didn't exactly help matters.

The bedroom door was driving me crazy. There was something about it that I wasn't grasping, something that didn't seem to fit.

Since my mind was way too wound up to think clearly, I decided to stop at Claude's house, to see if he could help me sort things out. He came to the door looking like he was auditioning for the lead role in the next sequel of "Night of the Living Dead."

"Did I wake ya?"

"No, I usually walk around looking like I'm still sleeping, asshole. Excuse me, Sergeant Asshole."

I followed Claude into the kitchen.

"Coffee?"

"I thought you'd never ask." I replied.

I sat down at his kitchen table, on one of the seats that gave me a full view of his perfectly landscaped backyard.

"I went to church this morning."

"What's the punch line, Max?" he asked as he filled up our coffee mugs.

"No punch line. Ken Vecchia called me this morning."

"You shitting me?"

"I shit you not. The woman came back to confession."

"Yeah, I'm listening."

"I spoke to her from the confessional booth, Ken's side of the booth, that is."

"Did you get her name?"

"No name. No face. But she was pregnant as all hell, that much I saw."

"What'd she have to say?"

"She worked with Lisa at North Shore. Lisa had told her

about those supposed dreams of hers. The woman thought there was more to it, though."

"Smart woman."

"She'd been to her apartment once."

"When?"

"Last winter. Do you remember how the bottom of the door was smashed in when we went there, on the day that she disappeared?"

"Of course I do. Why?"

"It was banged in like that when the woman was there last winter."

"She never got it fixed, I guess," Claude matter-of-factly replied.

"Yeah, but don't forget, it wasn't like that the first time that I was there."

Claude looked at me as if my third eye had again made its appearance. Then he stood up and skirted out of the kitchen. He reappeared in no time. A pair of blue jeans and a bright green short-sleeved shirt replaced the bathrobe that he'd been wearing.

"Let's go!" he yelled.

"Where are we going?" I yelled back as I once again followed Claude to his Ford Explorer without knowing where the hell we were heading.

CHAPTER 99

"Talk to me, partner," I said as Claude sped out of his neighborhood.

"When we were at her apartment that day, what did the super tell you?"

"Tell me about what?"

"About how he knows very little of Lisa Sanchez and about how he had so very little contact with her."

"I'm listening."

"Well, who the hell's been fixing the holes in her door?"

"Him, I assume."

"Then why didn't he mention it to us?"

"It probably slipped his mind."

"Don't you think that something like that would have rung a bell in his head, considering the fact that it was bashed in on the day that we were there?"

"What did he stand to gain by not making mentioning of it?"

"That's what we need to find out, Max! Think about it. How did he find out that it needed repair the first time? Did Lisa Sanchez call him and say, 'Could you please fix my bedroom door, I seem to have accidentally rammed my foot through it.' If it happened only once, maybe you could rule it an accident, like we had originally thought. But more than once? No way. Something's not right, Max. He didn't mention it for a reason."

It was at that very moment that I was struck with the realization that Claude was thinking much more clearly than me.

"I figured that would give you something to think about," Claude said as he glanced over at me.

A minute or two later, I heard him say, "If you bite down on that lip of yours any harder, I've got a feeling that you're going to chop it right off."

I didn't even realize that I was doing it. Biting my lip was something that I used to do all the time when I was a kid. It used to drive my mother absolutely crazy. "Max, stop biting your lip," my mom would tell me over and over again.

It was a nervous habit that I had rid myself of years ago. Its reoccurrence, I was certain, was not without just cause.

CHAPTER 100

When we arrived at the super's apartment, I landed a handful of good hard knocks on his door and then rang his doorbell a couple of dozen times.

There was no response. So I turned to Claude and said, "Ready?"

As Claude crouched down in his football stance, I pulled my gun out of my pants pocket. Then I stepped back and raised it, shoulder high.

Full force, Claude pounded his left shoulder into the door.

It didn't even budge.

He stood there, rubbing the top of his shoulder.

"This looks like a two-man job, Max."

So I slipped my pistol back into my pants pocket and stood beside him.

"Ready?" I asked.

Claude knelt back down into his stance. I followed suit. Then he gave the countdown.

"One, two, three, go!"

A loud, echoing thud followed our simultaneous leap into the door. The bark was much louder than the bite, though, because the door didn't swing open.

As I grabbed hold of the doorknob, however, I could feel that the lock had loosened. So I motioned for Claude to stand back and keep me covered.

As he stood there with his gun in hand, I lifted my right leg and slammed the heel of my foot smack into the door.

It flung wide open.

I turned to Claude and again made reference to the fact that we were entering someplace without a warrant by saying, "It's hard to believe that people still leave their doors wide open in this day and age."

When we stepped inside the pigsty, Claude said, "Holy shit! This place brings back memories of my college days."

"You figure a super would paint his own apartment once in a while," I replied as I looked around at the chipped-away paint on the walls and ceiling.

I headed towards the dresser, which stood beneath a large mirror at the other end of the small studio apartment. The dresser looked as if it hadn't been wiped clean since sometime in the prior century. The mirror, however, was sparkling clean.

I rummaged through the top dresser drawer.

Then, at the top of my lungs, I yelled, "Hey Claude, look what we have here!"

Claude hurried over to get a look at the photograph that I was holding.

"Holy Fucking Toledo!" Claude screamed as he caught sight of the photograph depicting the super holding a young toddler in his arms, with a beaming Lisa Sanchez standing there beside him.

"Look around some more. I'm going upstairs to her apartment."

CHAPTER 101

Full speed, I ran down the hallway and up the four flights of stairs.

I was huffing and puffing so heavily by the time that I made it to her apartment that I needed to take a two-second breather before tackling the task of getting her door open.

After a moment's rest, I slammed my shoulder into the door - nothing happened. So I tried it again - nothing. I was left with no choice, so I pulled my gun out of my pocket. Then I took a step back and blew the lock open.

Once inside, I immediately noticed that the bedroom door was closed, which is not the way that Claude and I had left it on our previous visit. So I hurried towards it.

With my gun drawn, I slowly opened the bedroom door.

The room looked a lot different, to put it mildly. The walls were painted black. The ceiling as well. And that was the least of it. On the wall, just above the bed, was a drawing of a tombstone, painted in stone-gray.

Its awkward, disproportionate design was clearly not the work of an artist. Its unglamorous artistry, however, in no way diminished its effect. It was the words written upon the tombstone that conveyed its horrifying message:

Here lies the body of Briana Rodgers.

Beloved soul mate of her twin sister, Briane.

November 12, 1999 to September 24, 2007

Sweet dreams, my child!

I yanked my cell phone out of my shirt pocket and called Claude's cell.

"Meet me at your truck, NOW!"

CHAPTER 102

By the time that I got outside, Claude was already sitting in his Explorer with the engine running. As soon as I hopped inside, he sped away. As he drove, I quoted the words that had been written upon Lisa Sanchez's bedroom wall.

"September 24th? That's today!" Claude yelled.

"No shit, Sherlock."

"Want to see my find?" Claude asked as he pulled a stack of photographs out of his shirt pocket and handed them to me.

They were photos of the victims.

I glanced through them without saying a word. Voicing my utter disgust would have served no constructive purpose at that point. So I placed them in the armrest compartment between our seats. Then I pulled out my cell phone and called Officer Gorman, who was patrolling the outside of the Rodgers' residence. He informed me that the Rodgers had left for church at around 9:15 that morning.

"Which church?"

"St. Matthews, on Merrits Blvd. Should I go there, to make sure that they're okay?"

"No. Stay right where you are and keep your eyes glued to the fucking house. Tell the others to do the same."

"What's going on?" Claude asked as I placed the cell phone back in my shirt pocket.

I explained the situation, which caused Claude to press his foot even further down on the gas pedal.

By the time that we pulled up in front of the church, the rain had finally stopped. Once inside, we headed straight to the chapel.

I walked over to the left aisle and Claude headed to the right.

Slowly, we made our way down our respective aisles, glancing down each row of pews as we passed them by. When I arrived at the front row, I took one last look around the place and then climbed up the four or five steps that led to the pulpit. The priest who stood there was a short, bald man with round, gold-rimmed glasses. He walked towards me as I approached.

With my back facing the congregation, I said, "I'm sorry to interrupt your service, Father, but we need to locate Mr. and Mrs. Rodgers and their daughter."

"My Lord! Are they okay?"

"Were they here earlier?" I asked, intentionally avoiding his question.

"Yes, they were in attendance at my 9:30 mass. They were seated in the front row, in the center. That's where they've been sitting every week since their daughter passed."

"What time did they leave here?"

"About eleven o'clock, when mass was over."

I glanced down at my watch. It was 11:37.

"You wouldn't happen to know where they went afterwards?"

In a voice that echoed the pained look on his face, he whispered, "No, I'm afraid that I don't."

CHAPTER 103

"Make-believe" had always been the twins' favorite game. Nothing was more fun for either of them than playing with playmates that could only be seen in their special little world.

As Briana sat, motionless, in the middle row of her parents' minivan, with her wrists tied in front of her, it was that very same game that her young, fragile mind had chosen to play. She made believe that Briane was sitting right next to her. She pretended as well that God had made an agreement with her: Briane would not have to return to Heaven if both she and her sister could hold back their tears until the man with the gun, sitting beside her, went away.

Her mom, seated in the passenger seat, was unable to play any such games. She was only able to see the horrifying reality of the situation. She tried many times to gain control of her emotions but her efforts proved fruitless. So as her husband drove onward, following the man's instructions of when to turn and in which direction, her tears flowed down her soaking wet blouse.

The rage that was brewing within Dan Rodgers had manifested itself within his grip on the steering wheel. With each passing moment, he became more and more enraged at the man seated behind him, the monster who savagely murdered his innocent, young daughter and who was now holding a gun to the head of her petrified twin sister.

CHAPTER 104

My heart was pounding a thousand beats a minute by the time that I called in the APB from the lobby of the church. That call immediately followed the one that I had made to Officer Gorman, in which he informed me that the Rodgers still hadn't returned home.

After we hopped aboard his SUV, Claude turned to me and asked, "What the fuck do we do now, drive around looking for them?"

Through the shrug of my shoulders, I let him know that I was feeling every bit as helpless as he was.

Then, just as we were about to pull onto the main road, I shouted, "Wait a minute!"

After his heart climbed back into his chest, Claude turned and looked at me.

"Do you remember where it was that Briane's body was found?"

"Somewhere off Exit 67 of the L.I.E. Why?"

"Because that's where he's taking them."

Claude looked right through me.

Then he flicked on the siren and put his foot to the pedal.

As we sped away, I called the precinct to get the exact location. Upon clicking off my cell phone, I said something to Claude that I'd never before felt the need to say.

"Better give it some more gas."

With the gas pedal flush to the floor, we made our way to the Long Island Expressway. When we got off at Exit 67, I told Claude to turn off the siren. Then, as he drove onward, I dictated the directions that had been relayed to me over the phone. Some minutes later, as we headed down an isolated, two-lane road, I instructed him to pull over and head in the direction of the heavily treed area that stood a couple of hundred yards to the north of us.

When we were a stone's throw from the woods, I told him to stop the truck and turn off the engine. Via the blatant look of confusion on his face, he asked me what was going on.

"We're making too much noise. We better walk it from here, to play it safe."

CHAPTER 105

With our hands raised in front of our faces to avoid having an eye poked out by a low-lying branch, I took lead of our journey into the woods. The dry leaves on the ground below caused me to slow down the pace a bit. The slower that we moved, the less pronounced was the loud, crackling noise that they emitted as our shoes stomped down upon them. The heavy rains had apparently failed to make it this far east.

With time being an ally of no one but our enemy, my moderate pace didn't last too long. Within a matter of minutes, we were doing a slow trot.

"Hey Max," Claude whispered loudly.

I turned around to look at him.

He was pointing at something up ahead. When he realized that I couldn't get my eyes in line with where it was that he was pointing to, he whispered, "There are tire tracks up ahead."

So I let him take the lead.

When we came upon the thick tracks, we followed their path, deeper and deeper into the woods. Then, just when I began to wonder which one of us would be the first to keel over from exhaustion, something up ahead forced us to stop dead in our tracks. Its bright red color left no doubt that the minivan, just barely within our view, belonged to the family of the late Briane Rodgers.

"Let's split up," I said.

Full speed, we ran towards the van from opposite directions.

What I saw as I drew closer is a sight that will forever be lodged in my mind. Briana was lying there, naked and shivering. She was tied down to a table. A thick rope dangled from the tree above. Her mom and dad were tied to the base of the tree next to her. A man with his back turned to me was standing above her, aiming some kind of object at her.

So I ran like hell to get closer, before it was too late.

Then, just as I was about to raise my gun, the man took a step back. It was then that I noticed that what he was holding was a camera.

As if it were someone else holding the pistol in my hand, I felt myself raise my gun and take aim at the back of his head. A split-second later, the man fell, face first, upon the earth.

I never got the chance to pull the trigger.

As I hurried over to them, I caught sight of Claude rushing towards them from the other direction.

After we made sure that there was no movement coming from the body, we untied the three of them.

They huddled together and wept.

We walked over to his body, lying there facedown. I put my right foot under his shoulder and turned him over.

The super, Jackson Tyler, a.k.a. "The Long Island Hangman," lay dead, his dark beady eyes still wide open.

"Did you see the way that he was getting ready to shoot her?" I asked.

"I couldn't let that happen. Could I, Max?"

"Well, I sure as hell wasn't about to just stand by and watch. Seems you beat me to the punch, by about a millisecond. I thought for sure that was a gun that he was holding."

"Me, too," Claude replied.

We reached out our oversized right hands and locked them firmly together as one.

"We got him, Max."

"We sure did, my friend."

Hours later, as we approached the precinct, we were caught off guard by what we saw: hundreds (and hundreds) of people gathered in front of it.

"Holy mackerel!" Claude yelled. Then he circled around the block, pulled into the parking lot from the side street, and parked right next to the rear entrance.

Once inside, we walked briskly down the hallway to the front entrance. Penny was standing there waiting for us.

She threw her arms around me.

"I love you," she whispered.

"I love you, too," I whispered back.

"Ready?" I asked.

"Ready or not," she replied.

"Hey, you're stealing my lines," I kidded.

Then I pushed the door open.

As soon as we stepped outside, the applause began. It wasn't a soft little round of applause either, but rather the kind that's usually reserved for rock concerts or sporting events.

People were shouting "thank you" and "God bless you" at the top of their lungs.

Penny broke down and wept. I put my arm around her as the three of us paraded down the steps. Tears were dripping down my face, Claude's as well. We were waving to everyone, just like a bunch of celebrities.

When we got to the bottom, the handshakes began. The last one came from Commissioner Kearney.

"Congratulations, Sergeant Miller. I can't begin to tell you how proud you've made all of us."

Then he turned to face the microphones.

His words were very brief.

"Ladies and gentlemen, it is my utmost pleasure to have Sergeant Max Miller speak on behalf of the Department."

I stepped up to the mass array of microphones, CNN, ABC, CBS, Fox and all of the local ones as well. The attractive blonde newscaster that I had seen on TV on the night that Claude was up at Bear Mountain was standing a few yards in front of me, along with a couple of dozen other reporters. Mobs of people were gathered behind police barricades.

The nervous tickle that somehow manages to find its way into my throat at times like this was nowhere to be found. The hot, glaring lights of the news cameras didn't bother me one bit either. They felt rather comforting, in fact, like that long-awaited ray of summer sunshine after a long, harsh winter.

I held up my hands to quiet the crowd. The smile on my face acknowledged their heartfelt ovations.

Then I said my piece.

"At approximately 1:30 this afternoon, the man who had come to be known as "The Long Island Hangman" was shot and killed by my longtime partner and close friend, Detective Claude Greer."

Claude bowed his head to acknowledge the crowd.

When the noise died down, I continued.

"His name was Jackson Tyler. He was from Flushing, Queens."

"It would take me hours to thank all those who deserve credit. So I'll limit it to those select few without whose help the killer would still be at large. First of all, I'd like to thank Dr. Penny Forrester for her invaluable insight in helping us solve the case. Without it, we would not be gathered here today. I'd also like to give a special thanks to Sister Rosemary for the courage she exhibited in helping to identify the suspect. My next set of thanks goes out to a woman who, for reasons unbeknownst to us, refuses to identify herself. I would like to assure this person that she has nothing to be afraid of or to be embarrassed about. I'd very much like the opportunity to thank her in person. As would a good many others, I'm sure.

"I saved the biggest thank you for the one who deserves it the most. He's a young lad named Derek Shiver. His sister, Tara, was one of the unfortunate victims. On the day that his sister was abducted, Derek made eye contact with the killer. You can just imagine how terrifying that must have been for a six-year-old kid. But Derek proved too brave a young man to let fear stand in his way for too long. On a Monday morning, Derek walked into my office, looked me straight in the eye and told me that he knew what the killer looked like. With the help of our top-notch artist, Katie Avero, a portrait of the suspect was circulated throughout the country.

"The very bravest one of all proved to be this six-year-old young man, Derek Shiver. By the way, Derek is a very big Yankee fan. So, all of you Yankee management people out there, please be sure to keep that in mind."

When the chuckles from the crowd died down, I concluded my speech in a much more somber tone of voice.

"In honor of my beloved mentor and good friend, the late Sergeant Earl Monahan, I have something I'd like to tell each and every one of our most cherished citizens.

"All is safe once again, our little ones."

Just like I promised, Sarge.

Chapter 106

Three Weeks Later

It was a Sunday morning just like any other. Penny and I were sprawled out in my living room, sipping our coffees and reading our newspapers, she on the couch, I in my easy chair.

Good old Sparky, who lay fast asleep on the floor beside me, let out a quick, loud bark when he heard the ring of the doorbell.

"Who the hell could that be?" I asked, making no attempt to move my fat derriere out of the chair.

"There's only one way to find out," Penny playfully replied.

We looked at each other and grinned.

Then I lifted myself out of my chair and did a slow walk to the front door, figuring it was some kid collecting money for his baseball team or soccer team, or something along those lines.

I was dead wrong! An attractive young lady wearing a nurse's uniform and holding onto a baby carriage was more like it.

As I pushed open the screen door, I got a better look at the woman's face and realized that she looked strikingly familiar.

"Life's too short to keep hiding behind veils," she said.

Upon hearing the sound of her undisguised voice, I stepped outside and wrapped my arms around her. We held each other tightly as we soaked one another with tears.

"Were you able to locate Lisa and Claudia?" she whispered.

"Not yet. But I'm not about to stop trying."

Then she looked down at her newborn child and said, "His name is Max. He's named after his grandpa, the hero."

I grabbed hold of the little guy and held him in my arms. Doing so brought a smile to my face the size of the Grand Canyon. Then I lowered him down and pulled open the screen door.

With that same shy grin sprawled across her adorable face, Jill stood on her toes and gave me a little peck on the cheek. Then she stepped forward to enter a place that she never even left.